Hickory Flat Public Library
2740 East Cherokee Drive
Canton, Georgia 30115

THE GREAT RAILROAD WAR

Center Point
Large Print

Also by Giles A. Lutz and available from
Center Point Large Print:

The Offenders
Wild Runs the River
The Grudge

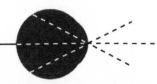

**This Large Print Book carries the
Seal of Approval of N.A.V.H.**

THE GREAT
RAILROAD WAR

Giles A. Lutz

CENTER POINT LARGE PRINT
THORNDIKE, MAINE

This Center Point Large Print edition
is published in the year 2016 by arrangement with
Golden West Literary Agency.

Frist US edition: Doubleday & Company, Inc.

The text of this Large Print edition is unabridged.
In other aspects, this book may vary
from the original edition.
Printed in the United States of America
on permanent paper.
Set in 16-point Times New Roman type.

ISBN: 978-1-62899-909-9 (hardcover)
ISBN: 978-1-62899-913-6 (paperback)

Library of Congress Cataloging-in-Publication Data

Names: Lutz, Giles A., author.
Title: The great railroad war / Giles A. Lutz.
Description: Center Point Large Print edition. | Thorndike, Maine :
Center Point Large Print, 2016. | ©1981
Identifiers: LCCN 2015049527| ISBN 9781628999099
    hardcover : alk. paper) | ISBN 9781628999136 (pbk. : alk. paper)
Subjects: LCSH: Large type books. | GSAFD: Western stories.
Classification: LCC PS3562.U83 G7 2016 | DDC 813/.54—dc23
LC record available at http://lccn.loc.gov/2015049527

CHAPTER ONE

Hell at its worst couldn't top an Oklahoma summer day. The heat wrapped around one like a heavy, stifling blanket until even thinking of drawing the next breath seemed a formidable chore. Men cursed the summer heat and prayed for the cold of winter. The next winter, they would curse the cold and pray for the return of summer.

This particular night, it seemed as though relief would never come. The sun had been down a good three hours, and while darkness had fallen over the town, energy was just as lacking as it had been earlier in the day.

Enid's usual evening traffic had slowed almost to a standstill. The streets were empty, and storekeepers stood in the doorways of their businesses, anxiously hoping for the arrival of customers. If this heat held on much longer, they would be ruined.

People kept close to their homes, sitting on the porch steps, listlessly talking about how long the heat would last. Just the thought of a short walk was unbearable. Ordinarily, men looked forward to a visit to a saloon to break up the monotony, but tonight the heat there would be stifling, and the lukewarm beer would only worsen it. There hadn't been any ice in town for the past week.

Six saloon girls sprawled uncomfortably on the chairs in the Palace Saloon. So far this evening there hadn't been a single customer, and every one of the women prayed it would continue that way. They fanned themselves, and every now and then lifted loose clothing in the hope that an errant breath of air would creep underneath.

Slim Trevlin, the barkeep and owner, looked over at the women, and their miserable appearance evoked a stir of pity in him.

"Why don't you gals go outside?" he called. "Maybe you can find a breath of air out there. Don't go too far, though. A customer might stray in."

Trevlin got several rude answers to his last proposal, but the women were grateful that Trevlin was letting them go out. "We appreciate it, Slim," two of them called back.

They walked outside and argued briefly about which side of the saloon to take. "There's only one bench," Ida Belle said, ending the argument. She was a nice-figured little blonde with a pert, pretty face. Tonight had played hell with her hairdo. The heat had made her perspire and the moisture had ruined her curls, making them hang limply about her face. "Why did I ever come to this miserable town?" she moaned.

A breeze sprang to life, making the sign

advertising the saloon swing over the walk. It creaked noisily. If there was anything palatial about the saloon it was only in Trevlin's mind.

"The same reason as the rest of us," Lily answered. "When the territory was opened, people flocked to it. Everybody heard there was a lot of money pouring into it. And we wind up working for Slim," she said scornfully. She was a big, brazen redhead with a bossy manner. Every now and then, her overbearing attitude got on the others' nerves. At times, she acted as though she was a goddess, and she was really no better than the rest of them.

Ida Belle sprang to the defense of Slim Trevlin. "We could work for worse bosses."

Lily sniffed. "Point out two reasons."

"Well, he put in this bench out here so we could use it. He let us off tonight."

"Hah!" Lily said triumphantly. "How many times have we used this bench? We're only using it tonight because there's no customers."

Ida Belle wilted under the irrefutable facts. "We could be working for a worse boss," she repeated weakly.

"I'd hate to have to go out and find him," Lily said spitefully.

A flash of temper showed in Ida Belle's eyes. Ordinarily, the six women got along well, for they knew the same common frustration, the same hopes, and the same inevitable dashing of spirit. Sometimes they quarreled bitterly, but it was usually over in a day or two.

"Anyway, it seemed like a good idea at the time," Ida Belle continued reflectively. "A new country with plenty of people rushing to it. When Congress gave the Rock Island Railroad a charter right to cross the Indian Territory in 1887, it opened up a land that hadn't been spoiled." She laughed, but it had a bitter ring. "I visualized this country filling up with men with money in their pockets. That's why I came. Besides, I was damned sick of St. Louis. Lily, you came here for the same reason I did: to help those people spend that money. You were just as wrong as I was. Enid and Pond Creek are nothing but hellholes. We fry in the summer and freeze in the winter."

Lily grinned. "I sure haven't gotten rich. But if you feel so strongly about it, why don't you go someplace else?"

Ida Belle's face tightened. "Are you telling me to get out?"

Lily's temper flared to meet Ida Belle's upsurge. "You're the only one complaining."

"Oh, cut it out," Maude said wearily. She was a gaunt brunette with too many years showing in her face. "The heat's talking for both of you. You keep this up and you'll be pulling hair. If that happens again, Slim will kick both of you out. Where would you go then?"

That frightened both of them, and it showed in

their faces. "Aw, come on, Maude," Ida Belle said petulantly. "We weren't quarreling. Like you said, it's just this wretched heat."

Lily bobbed her head in quick agreement. "It's bad enough to set Jesus' disciples to arguing." She flashed a bright grin at Ida Belle.

Ida Belle resumed fanning herself. It would make Slim mad if he knew what Ida Belle was thinking, but she was hoping to God that no customers came in tonight. Get a few drinks in them, and the customers thought they had the right to paw a saloon girl.

"If there was only something to do," she complained.

"There is for you," Lily announced, looking down the street. "If I'm not mistaken, here comes your Prince Charming."

The words swung Ida Belle's head around. Her eyes went wild. There was no mistaking the short, dumpy figure coming this way. Damn it, John Kevan was supposed to have left town this morning.

"Oh God," she moaned. "He's been in here the last four nights. I can't stand him again." The night before came back with a vividness that made it seem as though it was happening again. Kevan had an animal's lustiness; it never seemed to drain from him and Slim didn't do anything about it. Kevan was a big spender, and Slim wasn't about to lose a customer like that. She thought of jumping to her feet and fleeing, but it was too late. Kevan was too close. Surely he had spotted her.

Kevan forced his stumpy legs into a faster pace. "Hello there, sugar," he shouted. "I couldn't get last night out of my head. I decided to take another day off before I went back to work."

Ida Belle's jaw clenched. All she knew about Kevan was that he worked for the railroad somewhere in Chicago. It must be a pretty good job, for he spent lavishly. A year ago he had made a trip through Enid, spotted Ida Belle in the Palace, and returned every three months. Each time he had tipped her generously. But even the thought of those generous tips didn't change Ida Belle's thinking.

"One of you take him," she whispered frantically.

"I'd be glad to," Lily replied. "But you know he's only got eyes for you. You've bragged about his big tips." Lily couldn't resist rubbing Ida Belle's nose in her boasting.

Finally, Kevan reached her and looked down with a fatuous grin on his face. "Come on, sugar. We're wasting time."

Ida Belle shook her head. "Not tonight. It's too hot in there. Slim told us to go out and cool off. Maybe another time."

His eyes narrowed and turned mean. "This is my last night here for quite a while. You can't turn me down."

Ida Belle said adamantly, "I just don't feel up to it. Ask one of the other girls."

"I didn't lay over because of any of them. I want you."

Ida Belle got slowly to her feet. Kevan looked very angry, but she wasn't afraid of him. "It's still no, John. Not tonight. Last night, you said you'd be gone."

"I couldn't get last night out of my head, I told you. Damn it, that's a compliment. What's wrong with you? You always made money off of me."

Ida Belle's temper rose. This scene was turning ugly, and the girls were listening in fascination. This would give them something to talk about for days to come.

"I said no," she snapped and started to turn away.

Kevan grabbed her wrist and spun her around. "You can't turn me down like this," he grated. "Maybe I won't come back here again, but tonight I'm here."

Ida Belle was so angry she couldn't see clearly. "Let go of me. Because you spent a little money on me, you think you've bought and paid for me. You've got a few things to learn." She jerked her wrist free and swung the unhampered hand at his face.

Kevan ducked the slap, and Ida Belle had never seen a man so furious. "Why, damn you," he roared. He swung an openhanded slap of his

11

own. He had superior weight behind it and a greater fury propelling him. The slap caught Ida Belle on the cheek, rocking her head back, and she recoiled an unsteady step.

Ida Belle touched her burning cheek. The sting kept increasing, and she went wild.

"Why, you stinking—" she raved. Words spewed out of her mouth, and in her anger she wasn't sure of just what she said. She tore into him, her fingers hooked into claws. She caught his cheek with the left hand, and her long nails ripped flesh.

Kevan raised a hand to his stinging cheek, then looked at his bloodstained fingers. He howled and he sprang at her, chopping a short blow to her face. His rage destroyed his aim, however, and the blow landed high, glancing off her cheek-bone. But there was force to it—so much so that her eyes swam with tears of pain and rage. Her legs turned limber; she tried to retain her balance, but her muscles refused to coordinate and they buckled under her. She sat down hard, staring up at him. She was afraid she was going to bawl, and she bit her lips to forestall the tears.

"You rotten bastard," she screamed. "Just wait until I can get up."

"You don't have to, honey," Lily said. "We'll take care of what you have in mind."

All five women had risen and were advancing in a threatening line toward Kevan. His eyes rolled and he retreated. He didn't have any quarrel with them. He held out his hands in supplication. "Wait a minute," he pleaded. "You saw what she did to me. I don't have any quarrel with you."

"You made a bad mistake, mister," Lily purred. "Hitting one of us. You didn't think we could let that go by, did you?"

The line had spread out, and the ends were curving in on him. He was flanked on both sides now. His head jerked from side to side as he tried to keep their movements under surveillance.

"Don't try anything foolish," he warned, "or you'll be damned sorry." His voice kept going higher and higher, and it ended up on a squeak. He was going to have to slap some sense into their heads.

The center and the ends of the line rushed him all at once. Lily was in the center, and she reached Kevan first. He had tried to keep his attention on all of them, and he couldn't direct his blow very well. Lily ducked her head, and Kevan's slap missed her completely. She punched him in the mouth, and he felt his lips mash beneath the blow. He spat out blood.

Kevan tried to charge the next nearest woman, and a pair of stout hands fastened in his hair and yanked. It jerked him off balance, and before he could whirl to meet his latest attacker, one of the women kicked his feet from under him.

He went down hard, his face striking the dust. That hurt, and his mouth was filled with dirt. He tried to raise his head but his motions were dazed and uncoordinated. Rage overcame him. Punishing them wasn't enough; he wanted to kill every one of them.

Before he could rise, a horde of bodies slammed into him, throwing him back. Hands pummeled him, nails scraped at him, and his hair was savagely yanked again.

Kevan yelped under the punishment. For the first time, fear crept into his mind. Maybe he couldn't handle all of them. Maybe sheer numbers would overwhelm him.

Fear was a savage drag on his strength as he tried to gather a last remnant of power and throw them off. Oh God, there seemed to be more than five of them now. He would get rid of one, and three more seemed to take her place. There was nothing soft or feminine about these women. They were the Furies incarnate, and they were beating him into submission. He couldn't take any more of it. He had never known that women could be so primevally relentless. If somebody didn't come to his aid, he was going to be snowed under. He raised his voice and screamed for help. It might be disgraceful to admit his inferiority, but all he wanted was for somebody to yank these furious harpies off of him.

CHAPTER TWO

Jason Keeler rode slouched in the saddle. Even at a slow walk, windrows of sweat were piling up on the horse's withers. It was criminal enough to take poor Dandy out of the stable; now he would compound the affront by asking the animal for speed on such a stifling evening. Actually, he wasn't in that much of a hurry. April Budd didn't know he was coming, but he knew she would be there when he arrived. She was that type of woman. He closed his eyes, seeing again the fresh beauty of her. Jason remembered how his breath had caught the first time he had seen April. He had ridden into Enid on an errand a year ago, and the sight of her almost floored him. She had opened those sparkling gray eyes wide at being introduced to him, and it was like being hit with a club. She had the most desirable qualities of a woman. She could listen gravely to his serious discussion, but that bubbling humor showed when he made a light joke. Jason still didn't know how she had felt at that first meeting, but as for himself, he had never fully recovered. He had cursed the reason that had led him to Oklahoma, but after meeting her all that resentment was gone. April Budd was all the reason any man would want.

Jason had grown tired of his life in Chicago, and the news of vast reaches of land opening in Oklahoma had stirred him. As a result, he had joined the throngs packing the coaches to seek new roots.

He would never forget the seething hot day he arrived. Long before the forty-two-car train running south from Caldwell, Kansas, finally arrived in Oklahoma, Jason heard that another train was coming north from Hennessey. Both trains were filled with homeseekers.

But Jason wasn't after land; he was looking for a new site to establish his law office. He had read law under old Judge Garnet in Chicago, and he grinned lazily at the remembrance. What a tyrant that old man was! He detested slothfulness and carelessness, and he could bellow like an enraged bull. If a student did excellent work, however, Garnet would loosen up enough to issue grudging praise. Jason remembered the parting words between them.

"I don't know where you'll finally settle, Jason, but remember two things: Be honest in everything you do, and be eminently fair to every man who seeks your assistance, regardless of his worldly status. Keep that in mind, and you cannot fail."

Jason ruefully shook his head. He didn't doubt the veracity of the advice, and he had tried faithfully to practice it. But so far, he hadn't made a great success. In fact, he was struggling to get by.

He shrugged at the memory of the dull days while he waited for another client, then his eyes brightened. Meeting April had overcome all the dreary aspects of his trip into Oklahoma.

He recalled again the day of his arrival. He didn't know what the railroad had in mind, but the train had roared on by the land office in Enid. Hundreds of people had jumped from the coaches in the scramble to get claims. No one had been killed, but there were many a scraped knee and ripped trousers.

Actually, Jason hadn't really cared for the appearance of Enid and had gone on to the next town, Pond Creek. But the same thing happened again when the train failed to stop there.

Later, talking to a few old-timers, Jason found out what was going on. The government had planned on county seats in O and L counties, home of Enid and Pond Creek, respectively. The Rock Island Railroad had sneakily tried to control all the land surrounding these already established depots. No one could prove it, but railroad officials had met with Chief White Feather and sixty other tribal leaders. The Indians were supposed to select certain lands as part of the new treaty, and they would specifically choose lands adjoining the depots. Then they would sell the land to the Rock Island for whatever the railroad was willing to pay for a chance to speculate on the townsites. As it turned out, however, Secretary Hoke Smith in Washington got wind of the deal, and on the opening of the territory proclaimed that no county seat could be located within three miles of an Indian allotment. That was supposed to wreck the railroad's nefarious plans. Pond Creek and Enid would be located on the railroad as planned, but three miles south of each Rock Island depot.

The old-timers had chortled gleefully at the memory of the thwarting of the railroad's original plans. "That took a bite out of those bloodsuckers," one grizzled old man said happily. He splashed tobacco juice into the dust, but then his eyes turned stern. "It ain't all over yet, though. That puts the next move up to that damned railroad. Enid and Pond Creek will have to do something about this eventually, or those towns are doomed. How can a town grow without a depot?"

"You think there's more trouble ahead?" Jason asked.

"Plenty of it," the old-timer said morosely, "unless the leaders of Enid and Pond Creek get together and demand that the railroad either move its depots or stop trains at the government towns." He cocked an eye at Jason. "Young man, if you intend to grow with this community, you better get into the fight and see what you can do against the railroad."

Jason had taken that piece of good advice to heart and wormed his way into the group of leaders who were supposed to hold a talk with the Rock Island officials.

Delegations from Enid and Pond Creek met the railroad officials at Herington, Kansas. Jason could sense the animosity between the railroad and local civic leaders before a word was spoken. The railroad officials were a pompous group. They looked down their noses, and their arrogance stuck out all over them. These men were used to having their way. Jason had the sinking feeling that the local leaders were going to be chopped down before they fairly started.

Arnold Budd, the mayor of Enid, had made the towns' presentation. "We're asking the railroad to move its depots or stop the trains at the government towns. The present situation is impossible. It's stifling business and choking off the mail deliveries. Surely you can see that."

Budd was a plump-faced little man, and his good nature showed. He was trying to reach those arrogant men through reason. Jason knew it wasn't going to work. Budd wasn't impressive enough as a speaker, and he lacked the toughness to make the railroad officials feel he meant what he said.

A man named Ridings spoke for the railroad. "The Rock Island did extensive research before they decided where to place their depots. They carefully considered all phases, costs, and advantages of locations." Ridings paused and looked scornfully at these yokels. "You're asking us to build new improvements at locations only a few miles away from the established depots. We can't move the existing depots, and now you're asking us to wreck our schedules. What you ask would mean that we stop at new depots only a few miles farther down the tracks. Can't you see how impractical that would be?"

Budd's face grew redder as Ridings talked, and his lips quivered. "You mean you won't even consider our proposition?"

Up to this point Jason had remained silent, but now he had to step in. "Does the railroad intend to promote its own sites?" he asked quietly. Even with restraint his voice had carrying power. "Is the railroad going ahead selling allotments to settlers with the understanding that the railroad does not recognize the county seat towns, hoping that stand will draw people back to the original locations of the depots?"

Ridings flushed and chewed on his lower lip. Jason had asked a question he couldn't or didn't want to answer.

"Answer me!" Jason thundered. "These gentlemen have a right to know."

Ridings was at a loss for words, and he glanced helplessly at the group of leaders from Enid and Pond Creek.

Jason stabbed a finger at him. "Sir, what you're proposing means that two new towns will have to be built. That would mean a North Enid and a North Pond Creek. You'll be setting the new towns against the already established ones. Can't you see how much strife you'll be creating?"

"Does my esteemed opponent have the ability to see into the future?" Ridings sneered.

"I do when it comes down to something like this," Jason roared. "It would mean two more post offices. The government won't like that. The people in the new towns will naturally side in with the Rock Island Railroad. The older established towns will go along with the government. The matter won't be settled quietly. Quarrels will spring up, and bloodshed will follow. Is that what the railroad wants?"

Ridings alternately flushed and paled. He breathed gustily, and his eyes were wild. "Sir," he yelled, "you're meddling in something that doesn't concern you."

Jason chuckled. "I think it does. I live in Pond Creek. What happens there concerns me in every way."

"The discussion is over," Ridings said coldly. He motioned to the other railroad representatives and stalked away, leading the group. With his chest puffed out, he looked like an angry Bantam rooster.

"You whipped them," Budd said and whacked Jason on the back.

"I didn't whip anybody," Jason disagreed. "All I did was stir them into greater action. I don't know what inducements the railroad will offer, but you'll see North Enid and North Pond Creek spring into life."

"Can anything be done to stop them?" Budd asked with a distressed expression.

"Maybe one thing. We can petition the government to order the Rock Island to leave mail at South Enid and Pond Creek."

"Will you take care of it?" Budd begged.

Jason started to refuse, then reconsidered. As long as he had gone this far he might as well go all the way.

"I'll write a letter to Washington," he agreed as the rest of the town leaders gathered around, "and tell the government what is going on. Maybe when the Rock Island finds out it is fighting the govern-ment and not two small towns things will improve."

Jason had never heard such enthusiastic approval. He was afraid he was going to be hoisted onto their shoulders. Poor people, he thought sadly. Their hopes ebbed and flowed at the slightest change in the current. The letter wasn't even written yet, and here they were acting as though it was a great victory.

One good thing happened from his speaking out. He was no longer anonymous. By stepping into local politics he became well known.

Shortly after that he met April, at a church social.

"I know your father," he had told her at the meeting.

"Yes," she acknowledged. "Papa has talked a lot about you. He thinks you're wonderful."

Jason grinned. He wished he dared to say that he hoped it was the daughter's opinion and not the father's.

Soon, things began breaking his way. People he had never seen before made it a point to visit his office in Pond Creek and talk over the coming war with the railroad. It took considerable time to talk to them, but it was to his advantage. Quite a few people brought him new business.

He was just entering the outskirts of South Enid, and his pulse beat more rapidly. Although April wasn't expecting him tonight, he was sure she wouldn't resent his visit. Her welcome the last few times he had seen her had grown warmer. His own feelings had grown to such an extent that he would use any pretext to see her.

He dismounted before the modest home and walked up to the door. He knocked on it, and his heart echoed in rhythm with his knuckles.

His face fell as the door opened. Arnold Budd answered his knock.

"Jason," Budd exclaimed, grabbing for his hand. "Come in, come in."

Jason couldn't quite match the enthusiasm. "Arnold, I came to see April."

"She isn't here," Budd said regretfully.

Jason tried to keep his crestfallen spirits from showing. "She isn't out with another—" He gulped and cut off the last word. Saying "fellow" would reveal his true feelings.

Budd caught it, and he chuckled. "She isn't, Jason. You should know by now she's got eyes only for you. She's visiting her aunt in the country for the weekend. I'm sorry."

Not half as sorry as Jason was, although it wasn't really shattering news. At least no other man had caught her attention. "I'll come back again, Arnold."

"Sit for a while," Budd begged. "Any more news from Washington?"

"No more than the first answer I showed you. I wrote another letter asking for more information."

"They sure take their time," Budd fretted.

Jason grinned. "Expect that whenever you're dealing with Washington."

"More people are slipping away to the new town," Budd fumed. "I guess the railroad is making it profitable for them. I'm telling you it's going to be one hell of a fight before it's settled."

"The same thing is happening at Pond Creek, Arnold. You expected this from the start, didn't you? Quit worrying. We'll win in the end."

Budd's expression was lugubrious. "I hope you are right."

Jason grinned again. "You'll have to wait and see."

Budd wanted to talk some more, but Jason shook his head. There was really nothing to talk about except hopes and fears, and both could be dreary subjects.

"I've got some beer." Budd tried to entice Jason further.

Jason declined. The beer would probably be warm. "No, I'd better be getting back, Arnold. I've got some paperwork to catch up on. Tell April I was here. I'll be back as soon as I can."

Budd walked with Jason to the door. "I'll do that, Jason. She'll be sorry she missed you."

Jason shook hands again with Budd and walked to his horse. He tried to shake off his irritation. He couldn't expect to have the total say-so about April's activities—not for a while anyway.

He mounted and turned Dandy. The prospects of going back the same way weren't enticing, particularly at the same slow pace he had come, so he altered his course a couple of blocks. That would take him by the Palace Saloon, and he looked forward to seeing Ida Belle again. He had seen her occasionally before April came into his life. That was in what he liked to think of as his younger, hot-blooded days. Of course, he would never want April to know about it, but he wasn't really ashamed. He was footloose then, and he had wandered all over town. Ida Belle was fun to know, and he had enjoyed her bubbling sense of humor. Jason thought she was fond of him, too. If he went into the saloon tonight, it would be only for a brief visit. He would say hello to her and be on his way.

He turned the corner, and the saloon was just ahead. The moonlight wasn't strong, but he could see some kind of a commotion going on outside. Jason stood in the stirrups to get a better view. It looked as though a fight was going on there, but that couldn't be right, for Jason saw flashes of women's dresses. He heard feminine curses, pitched high and filled with passion.

Jason smirked as the solution came to him. The saloon girls were in some kind of a fight. He imagined that happened occasionally, and he could understand it. Their lives were dull and monotonous, and it was surprising that these fights didn't happen more often. The release of pent-up passions might be a good way to throw off stress. He was amazed that Trevlin wasn't out there trying to break it up, but maybe he was so used to these female tantrums that he gave them no credence and let them wear out of their own weight.

He was almost up to the threshing pile of bodies when one figure stood up. Her hair was down, and her dress hung in tatters.

"Damn you, John Kevan," she screamed and plunged back into the fray.

Jason knew that voice well; it was Ida Belle. But this wasn't a female fight. At least one man was involved. He didn't know what it was all about, but he'd better stop this before somebody got hurt. The name John Kevan meant nothing at all to him, but if a man was involved, he appeared to be getting the worst of it.

CHAPTER THREE

Ida Belle was so angry that for a moment she didn't recognize him.

"Whoa, Ida Belle," he said as he hauled her out of the fray. "It's Jason."

She stared wide-eyed at him, and the fury slowly left her eyes. "Jason," she whimpered. "Am I glad to see you!"

She came into his arms, and he wrapped them about her. This was no trick of feminine guile; it was the instinctive gesture of a wounded creature seeking protection.

"What's this all about?" he demanded.

That put a flare of temper back into her eyes. "That lousy John Kevan," she said heatedly. "Because he's been here before, he thought he owned me. He works for the railroad. When I refused to talk to him tonight, he knocked me down."

"The hell he did," Jason exploded. He didn't doubt Ida Belle. Even in his brief experience with her, he had never known her to lie or shade the truth, even if it was to her advantage. "Maybe we can straighten him out."

He started forward, then stopped. "What are the other girls doing in this?"

"They didn't like him hitting me," Ida Belle said simply.

Jason grinned. "Looks like he picked the wrong herd of females to corral. I don't like it, either."

He stepped up to the pile of bodies. He had never heard such abusive language. These gals knew every word a man knew, but they used them with more venom. Coming from softer lips made the language more shocking.

He grabbed the first arm he could reach and pulled one of the women aside. She struggled to return to the fight, and he had to shake her to make her recognize him. "Hey, Lily," he protested. "It's Jason. I'm on your side."

He chuckled as she shook herself and sanity returned to her eyes. She must have been in the midst of this fray, for her face was scratched and bruised and her hair was in wild disarray. This Kevan hadn't really shown up yet. Four other female bodies covered him, and they flailed away with their fists, pummeling every part of him they could see.

Lily looked down at the ruin of her dress and sobbed, but it wasn't a sign of female weakness. It was an expression of rage and unhappiness. "Look what that worm did to my dress," she said heatedly.

She wanted to get back into the struggle, but Jason said, "No! I'll take care of him."

He pulled one kicking, bucking female after another from the pile, and Lily and Ida Belle restrained them. Kevan was the last one he uncovered. He was down on his hands and knees, trying to protect his head with his arms. The women had thoroughly whipped him, and he had given up.

Jason shook his head in disgust. What a noble sight Kevan made, a man cowering before the onslaught of women. Jason kicked him in the rear with all the force he could muster.

The kick jolted Kevan a couple of feet along the ground, and he howled with pain and the affront to his dignity. Then he raised himself to his knees and looked around. His face was a mess. Scratches crosshatched it, and the discolorations of bruises were everywhere. His clothing was bloodstained and dirt-soiled. Jason guessed this man had been pushed to his limits of physical and mental endurance.

Kevan screamed, and the high, shrill sound verified Jason's assumption. This man was shoved near the verge of collapse. "What was that kick for?"

"For being manly enough to try and whip a bunch of females," Jason said calmly. "Get up."

Kevan struggled to his feet and looked around at the gloating women. "You didn't kick any of them," he complained. "They jumped me. They started this."

"You're a liar," Ida Belle said hotly. "You hit me. The girls jumped in only to protect me."

"All of you are lying harpies," Kevan yelled. "I'm going to make every one of you sorry. You'll see—"

Jason hit Kevan on the shoulder, spinning him around. He was a head taller than this dumpy figure and had broader shoulders and a deeper chest. "Stop that kind of talk," he ordered.

"What kind of a man are you?" Kevan asked contemptuously, "turning against your own sex?"

"I hope I never sink as low as you have," Jason said savagely. He wanted to goad Kevan into violent action, this time against him.

"You can't talk to me like that," Kevan screamed.

"Do something about it," Jason invited.

Kevan hesitated, then his face fired. He rushed at Jason and swung a wildly aimed fist.

Jason easily blocked the blow, then sank his left fist into the pudgy stomach. The force of the blow whooshed the breath out of Kevan. He doubled over, wrapping his arms about the abused area. His chin was then completely unprotected, and Jason swung at it. He got all his shoulder muscles behind the blow, and Kevan's head snapped back, straightening him up. The sound of the blow was a dull, soggy thud, and Kevan flailed his arms about in an effort to retain his balance. It was a losing battle, for he kept stumbling backward. He went back a good yard before he sank to the ground. He groaned, made a last feeble effort to rise, then all the strength went out of him. His head flopped back into the dust and his eyes went blank.

The girls rushed toward Jason to congratulate him. "You sure knocked the fight out of him," Ida Belle said triumphantly.

"This is the only time I wish I was a man," Lily remarked.

Jason cast her an amused glance. "Why's that?"

"To have enough muscle to shut up a big-mouthed braggart like that," she said viciously.

"But otherwise you wouldn't change," Jason said.

"Hell no," she answered emphatically. "What are you going to do with him?"

"Me? Nothing. Will one of you go find the sheriff and ask him to come up here? I'll keep an eye on Kevan until you come back."

"Do you think the sheriff will throw him in jail?" Lily asked.

"I think you can bet on it," Jason replied. "Go on now and find him."

Lily turned and hurried down the street. For a gal who had just been engaged in a bruising scrap, she moved pretty well.

Ida Belle wrapped her hands about Jason's bicep. "You know, I'm glad you came along, Jason."

Jason patted the hands. "You know, I am too."

Lily must have known where to find the sheriff, for in less than ten minutes she was back with a blocky man in tow. Kevan was just beginning to return to consciousness, rolling his head about and moaning softly.

"This is Sheriff Wheeling," Lily introduced the law official. "This is Jason—"

"I know Jason Keeler," Wheeling interrupted. "We've worked together a few times." Wheeling was a huge man, built on the lines of a wooden block. As big as Jason's hand was, Wheeling's encompassed it in a hearty handshake. "You been around making trouble, counselor?"

Jason smiled. "Didn't Lily tell you what happened?"

"She said you hit and knocked out a man. I'm here to learn the reason."

Trevlin picked that moment to come out of the saloon. He was a painfully thin man in his fifties with deep lines in his face.

Kevan was struggling to sit up, and Trevlin exclaimed, "What's been going on here? That's John Kevan. He's been a good customer."

Kevan got his eyes focused, and they rested on Jason. "Arrest that man," he yelled shrilly. "He hit me for no reason at all."

Jason began to get angry. "Lily, didn't you tell the sheriff anything about this?"

"I thought I'd let him see for himself." She grinned at Trevlin's glare. "Anyway, Slim, Kevan knocked Ida Belle down because she refused to pay him any mind tonight. All the girls piled in to teach Kevan that he couldn't treat one of us that way."

Trevlin's mouth sagged open, and he looked at all the hard, accusing faces. "I didn't know," he faltered. He didn't like being put in this awkward spot, and his temper rose. "Damn you, John Kevan. Don't you ever come back here again."

Kevan had gotten to his feet. "Do you think I'd ever want to come back to this crummy joint?" he sneered. He turned to leave.

"Whoa," Wheeling said. "You don't get off that easy. You got anything to add, Lily?"

"We piled into him for mishandling Ida Belle." Her sniff was eloquent. "He wasn't much. We could have taken care of him. We didn't need Jason. The next thing I knew, Jason was pulling us off him."

"That true, Jason?" Wheeling queried.

"Just about," Jason admitted. "When I got down to Kevan, he was hunkered up like a baby hunting cover. I couldn't resist kicking him."

Wheeling laughed until he cried. He wiped his eyes and said, "Good for you. He resented that kick?"

"He must have. He swung at me, but I blocked

34

the blow and hit him in the belly, then on the chin. That knocked him cold, and Lily went after you." Jason shrugged. "That's about all there is to it." Then his face hardened. "I don't think he should get off scot-free, though. Look at the girls' dresses. Every one of them is ruined. I think he should have to replace them." He flashed an amused glance at Trevlin. "Unless Slim wants to buy new ones."

Trevlin opened and closed his mouth like a fish out of water. "Wait a minute," he squalled. "I didn't have anything to do with this."

"Maybe this teaches you to look around before you jump into something you don't know anything about," Lily said bitingly.

Wheeling winked at Jason. "He's not getting away scot-free. I'm locking him up tonight and preferring charges of disturbing the peace." He pulled a pair of handcuffs from his hip pocket and snapped them on Kevan's wrists, clearly amused by the whole incident. "Can't take chances with such a dangerous man."

Kevan howled in indignation as he looked at his pinioned wrists. "You can't do this to me. Don't you know who I am?"

"Suppose you tell me," Wheeling said calmly.

"I work for the railroad. I can make it rough—" Kevan broke off suddenly and looked uneasily around.

"Go ahead," Wheeling said.

Kevan sullenly shook his head. "You'll find out. You'll be sorry."

Jason's eyes sharpened. He wondered if Kevan had an important job with the Rock Island. If so, a lucky cast of his net had caught him a bigger fish than he had imagined.

Wheeling shoved Kevan ahead of him. "Come on. You're going to jail."

Kevan's jaw was set hard. "I'll make you bloody sorry for this. Yes, I'll make Enid sorry, too."

"You scare the hell out of me," Wheeling said in mock terror. "Don't forget the man who knocked you out. He's from Pond Creek."

Kevan turned a belligerent face toward Jason. "I won't forget him, either. Before I'm through, both of you will be sorry you were born." He swept the group of women with savage eyes. "That goes for all of you, too."

Wheeling laughed uproariously. "Doesn't that frighten all you gals? Jason, I expect to see you in court tomorrow morning."

"Why me?" Jason asked in surprise. "I've got some work to catch up on in Pond Creek. I can't—"

"You will," Wheeling said unmoved. "You'll be there, or I'll come after you. You're an important witness in this case. He'll come up before Judge Kilmore in the morning. You know how the judge is. He won't stand for anybody being late in his court."

Jason couldn't buck these odds, and he gave in. "I'll be there. How about the girls? Do you want them?"

Wheeling surveyed the women with twinkling eyes. "They might make the case go a little harder against Mr. Kevan. See all of you in court."

Jason swore softly as he watched Wheeling march Kevan away. Then he had an idea as he looked at the women. "You girls wear the same clothes to court."

Lily started shaking her head, and Jason said softly, "It might help things go a little harder on Mr. Kevan. If I know Judge Kilmore, he'll be pretty unhappy about the whole matter. It might help you get the cost of new dresses out of Kevan." He grinned at the tickled burst of laughter coming from the women.

"That won't make you the heavy, Jason," Ida Belle said happily.

"I'm thinking of having to ride back to Pond Creek, then returning in the morning. It hardly seems worthwhile." He shook his head disconsolately at the prospects. Oh, he could rent a room at Enid's hotel, but that wasn't appealing either.

"I wish my room was bigger," Ida Belle said.

Jason wondered if some memory were prodding her. "Forget it, Ida Belle. I'll get a room at the hotel."

"I'm sorry for being so forward, Jason."

"I haven't forgotten a thing, Ida Belle, but things just aren't the same as they used to be."

She stared at him, her eyes sad. "It's the same girl, isn't it, Jason?"

"The same one," he said steadily.

"I saw her several times. She's a beautiful woman."

Jason smiled. "Don't I know it."

"She's a very lucky woman," Ida Belle said and started to turn.

Jason grabbed her and kissed her on the forehead.

"What was that for?" she asked in mild surprise.

"For old memories. For being quite a gal yourself."

She angrily brushed at her eyes, and Jason suspected tears were close to leaking out. "Good night, Jason." Her voice was quite firm.

He stood there watching her until she disappeared into the Palace. He cleared his throat. What would become of her? He didn't know. "Oh, damn it," he said helplessly. "Ida Belle— wait!"

CHAPTER FOUR

It was amazing how news got around in such a short time. The courtroom was packed. Jason recognized a reporter from the local newspaper. Who had spread the news that an interesting case was coming up? He shrugged. For the life of him, he didn't have the slightest idea.

Wheeling brought Kevan in, and Jason had never seen a more dispirited man. The night in the local jail hadn't done him the least bit of good. His clothing was rumpled, and his hair was disheveled. He hadn't been able to do much about the scratches on his face. If anything, they were worse, for the discoloration showed up more plainly.

Wheeling led Kevan to a small table in front of the room and motioned for him to sit down. A paunchy man with a balding head was already seated at the table. That was Wilbur Stasson, the public defender, and Jason didn't think much of him; if he were ever in any kind of a scrape, he wouldn't want Stasson for a lawyer. He even felt a little pity for Kevan. Stasson had a long list of failures.

Stacey Tillman was the prosecuting attorney, and Jason rated him as a sharp one. He had talked to Tillman before he entered the courtroom, filling him in on the details of the fight. Tillman had listened attentively.

"You brought the girls in?" Tillman had asked. At Jason's nod he said, "Good. That Kevan is a dead duck even if he doesn't know it yet. I'd like nothing better than to smash any of the Rock Island workers. They think they're a cut better than anybody."

"Will Kilmore give Kevan extra consideration because of his connection with the railroad?" Jason asked.

Tillman snorted. "You don't know the judge very well. He's pretty hot already because of the high-handed way Rock Island is handling this matter." He glanced over at Kevan, and his smile looked a little cruel. "I wouldn't want to be in that one's shoes."

Jason grinned and sat back to enjoy himself.

Judge Kilmore came in. The old black robe made him look dumpier than usual. He was a short man with sagging jowls, and the light shone from his burnished pate.

"The honorable Judge Kilmore," the bailiff announced. "Everybody stand."

The six girls stood off to one side, and Jason winked at them. Small, triumphant smiles played on their faces. Perhaps their intuition told them how this trial would go.

Kilmore cleared his throat. "Announce the next case, Bailiff." He lacked height and was too plump to look formidable, but his face was stern. He could be a tough judge.

"The city of Enid against one John Kevan. He is accused of disturbing the peace."

Kevan jumped to his feet. "I didn't disturb the peace, your honor. I was only protecting myself."

"One more outbreak like that, Mr. Kevan, and I'll fine you for contempt of court. Sit down!"

A titter ran through the room. Kilmore banged furiously with his gavel. "This court will not stand for any demonstrations like that. Another outbreak, and I will order the courtroom cleared. Is that understood?" The bald head slowly turned as fierce eyes scanned the room.

Jason kept his face stolid, even though he wanted to laugh. He wondered if Kevan had any insight of what was ahead for him.

"Mr. Tillman, proceed with your case," Kilmore said.

Tillman stood and said, "I call Sheriff Wheeling."

Not a nerve showed in Wheeling as he took the witness chair. It shouldn't, for he was an old veteran of courtrooms.

The bailiff swore him in, and Tillman said smoothly, "Proceed with your knowledge of this affair."

"Last night, Lily rushed in yelling that man—" Wheeling jerked his head at Kevan "—was beating up on Trevlin's girls. I asked if he was drunk, and she said, 'No, just mean.'"

That started another trickle of laughter, but the spectators remembered Kilmore's threat and quickly stifled their merriment.

Kilmore glared at the suddenly quiet room, and the spectators stared owl-eyed back at him. "Proceed, Mr. Tillman," he snapped.

"Was the fight still in progress when you arrived, Sheriff?" Tillman continued.

Wheeling shook his head. "It was all over when I got there. Kevan was on the ground, unconscious. Jason stood over him."

Tillman was a good actor, for he pretended amazement. "What did Jason have to do with this affair?"

"I don't know," Wheeling said blandly. "Perhaps he can tell you."

"Any cross-examination?" Kilmore asked of Stasson.

Stasson shook his head. He had had run-ins with the sheriff before. When Wheeling told a story, nobody could shake it.

"The witness is dismissed," Kilmore said. "Call Mr. Keeler."

Jason took the chair. None of this bothered him. As long as he kept his story straight and clear, it couldn't be shaken.

"Were you at the scene, Mr. Keeler?" Tillman asked.

"Not as a customer, sir. I just happened to be riding by the saloon when I saw the six ladies struggling in a pile on the ground. There was a lot of screaming and quite a bit of cursing. Whatever was happening surely had those ladies worked up."

Tillman echoed Jason's ghost of a smile. "Go on," he said quietly. "Have you been a regular patron of the saloon?" Tillman asked.

Jason didn't want to answer that question. There was a reporter in the courtroom, and his reply could easily get into the paper. He remembered Judge Garnet's advice, "Be honest and fair." It was best he stick to it regardless of the consequences.

"When I first came to Pond Creek," he went on, "I was young and lonely." He spread his hands eloquently and stared impassively at Tillman. He knew what the prosecutor was trying to do: establish a background for the rest of Jason's story to bolster its credibility.

Tillman's eyes twinkled. "Go on, Mr. Keeler."

At least Tillman was satisfied, Jason thought as he picked up the story. "Anyway, I asked Ida Belle what was happening, and she told me the ladies were fighting with Mr. Kevan because he knocked Ida Belle down when she refused to see him that evening."

Kilmore banged with his gavel, cutting off any attempt at laughter before it started. He glared long and ominously at Kevan before he said, "Continue."

Jason cleared his throat. "The ladies had gone to Ida Belle's aid, and they were whipping Mr. Kevan. I had to pull them off of him." His lips twitched at the memory of the scene, and he almost broke into laughter.

"Yes?" Kilmore said patiently.

"Mr. Kevan was down on his hands and knees, his arms wrapped about his head as though he was trying to protect it. I booted him in the rump to help him get to his feet. That seemed to help him," Jason said dryly. "He lost his head and swung at me. I knocked him cold, then sent for Sheriff Wheeling. The sheriff came up just as Kevan regained consciousness. That's all of my part in this."

"Your witness, Mr. Stasson," Tillman said.

Maybe Stasson didn't realize it, but there was a suggestion of a strut in his walk as he approached Jason. "Is there a personal animosity between you and Mr. Kevan?" he purred.

Jason carefully considered the question. This man was laying some sort of a clumsy trap for him. After a moment's deliberation he said, "There couldn't be. I never saw Mr. Kevan before in my life."

"Aha!" Stasson shouted, and triumph rang out in the word. "Then you make it a habit of going to the aid of ladies of shady reputation?"

Tillman was on his feet, protesting loudly. "The reputation of these ladies isn't in question. To go into that question thoroughly would take days in this court."

"Objection sustained," Kilmore barked.

Stasson wilted under the adverse ruling for a moment, then pressed on. "But you did go to the help of these—" he managed to put a sneer into his voice "—ladies?"

"I'd go to the help of any ladies if they were being abused by a male."

Kilmore glared about the room, daring someone to try and make something out of that. He looked back at Stasson. "Any more questions?"

Stasson didn't move his hands, but the expression on his face gave the impression that he wanted to throw them into the air. "No more questions, your honor." He had failed to tear Jason down, and the sulky tone of his voice acknowledged it.

Jason stepped down, and Tillman winked as he passed.

"I call Ida Belle," Tillman said.

Ida Belle tossed her head perkily as she took the chair. She let her baleful eyes rest on Kevan before she looked at Tillman.

The bailiff swore her in, and Tillman asked for her occupation.

"I work for Slim Trevlin at the Palace Saloon," Ida Belle answered. If there was any shame in her voice, it wasn't apparent.

"You've seen Mr. Kevan before?"

Ida Belle crinkled her brow. "Yes. He's been in the Palace a number of times."

"How many times?"

Ida Belle's frown increased. "Several. The last time he was in town, he came in four straight nights."

"Then you would consider him a good customer?"

"I did until last night."

"You refused to treat him like a good paying customer last night?"

"I did." Her voice was tough. "Last night was so awfully hot—" She glanced hastily at Judge Kilmore. "Your honor, I don't have to tell you how beastly hot it was."

The judge's frosty façade almost cracked. "It was," he agreed. "And it looks as though tonight will be another of the same. Continue."

"It was so hot in the saloon that Slim told all of the girls we could go outside. There were no customers, and we were grateful for a chance to get a breath of fresh air."

She paused, frowning as though she wanted to get her story correct. "Then John Kevan came up. He wanted me to go inside and drink with him. When I refused, he got rough with me. You can still see the marks on my face. I don't usually go around with my hair looking like this. I left it this way so the court could see what he did to me. He acted like I was some kind of slave. I lost my head and slapped him. That drove him wild. He hit me on the cheekbone and knocked me down. That's when the other girls piled on him. I did the same when I recovered enough to get back on my feet."

Tillman coughed to hide his tendency to laugh. "That's all, Ida Belle. Unless Mr. Stasson wants to question you."

"You bet I do," Stasson growled. He approached her as though he was stalking game. "Do you saloon girls make so much money that you can afford to turn down a customer who had proven he was generous, only because the night was hot?"

Tillman was on his feet, objecting strenuously. "Your honor, I don't think Mr. Stasson has any right to ask questions like that."

"Sustained, Mr. Tillman."

"I don't think these ladies, as the judge insists on calling them, have many hidden secrets," Stasson said stubbornly.

Tillman started to object, and Kilmore waved him quiet. "That'll be enough of that, Mr. Stasson. You've been warned. Keep on, and you'll be fined for contempt of court."

Stasson gulped and looked helplessly at Ida Belle. "Do you have anything to say that might help clear this up?"

Ida Belle bridled under Stasson's manner.

"Mr. Kevan had been generous in the past," she admitted. "It wasn't that, and it wasn't solely the heat. It was the way he thought he owned me. No man hits me without me trying to get even with him."

Stasson stood there, his mouth opening and closing.

"It's evident you haven't anything else to say," Kilmore said coldly. "The witness may step down."

A small wave of applause ran through the room as Ida Belle left the stand. She hadn't lost any consideration with this audience.

Kilmore frowned. He hadn't warned them against applauding, and he didn't comment. "Any more witnesses, Mr. Tillman?"

"Several, I'm afraid, sir. And I certainly want to question Mr. Kevan."

"Get on with it," Kilmore said wearily.

Tillman called Lily to the chair. She told essentially the same story as Ida Belle. "Look at my dress," she cried. "I won't have any bast—" she gulped and caught the word "—any man, no matter how big he thinks he is, hurting my friend."

"Did you need Jason?" Tillman asked.

Lily glanced judiciously at Jason. "I don't think so. He just helped end it earlier."

"That'll do, Lily, if Mr. Stasson has no questions."

Stasson shook his head, staring frozenly ahead. All these women would tell the same story.

Tillman called all six of the women, and indeed their stories didn't vary.

"I call Mr. Kevan," Tillman announced finally. He purred like a kitten at a fresh saucer of cream.

The bailiff swore Kevan in, and Tillman asked in that same silky voice, "What is your occupation, Mr. Kevan?"

"I work for the Rock Island Railroad."

"Can't you pin it down closer? Are you an engineer, a flagman, a conductor?"

"It doesn't matter." There was anger in Kevan's face.

"You don't sound very proud of your job."

"It's better than this stinking town can offer," Kevan flared.

Tillman glanced at Jason and raised his eyebrows. He was indicating to Jason a point to remember.

"The Rock Island Railroad," Tillman repeated. "Imagine that. The same railroad that's brought grief to Enid and Pond Creek. Do you have anything to do with the railroad's policy?"

Stasson was almost screaming as he jumped to his feet. "What Mr. Kevan does is not germane to this case."

"It may be, your honor," Tillman said. "Anything the railroad does or will do could hurt Enid and Pond Creek in the future."

"I'm inclined to agree with you," Kilmore said. "Proceed, Mr. Tillman."

"Your offices are in Chicago, aren't they, Mr. Kevan? Did you have to come to Enid to find your pleasure? I believe that was often, wasn't it?"

He hit a sore nerve, for Kevan squirmed.

Tillman was a good lawyer, Jason thought. He had backed Kevan into a corner and was rapidly squeezing it in on him.

"I came down here on business," Kevan said, his eyes riveted on the floor. "I just happened to run across Ida Belle."

Jason watched him curiously. Kevan wasn't one of the rank-and-file Rock Island employees. His clothing and attitude attested to that. And he seemed mortally terrified of something coming out of this trial. Was it a worry over his job, or was his private life involved? It was an interesting question, and Jason filed it away in his mind for future use.

"How many times did you run into Ida Belle?" Tillman proceeded relentlessly.

Kevan pulled at his fingers. "How would I know? I've got more important things on my mind than to be concerned with such trivia."

Tillman's fangs showed. "It is odd that a big, important man like you has such a faulty memory. Ida Belle says you have come in several times. Was she right?" He hammered the question at Kevan.

Kevan's agitation became more apparent. "I told you I don't remember."

Tillman opened his hand as though he was letting something fall to the floor. "We'll let that go for now, Mr. Kevan. Do you get a satisfaction out of abusing women?"

That stung Kevan. He raised his head and howled. Stasson was on his feet.

Jason whistled inwardly. Tillman was tearing Kevan's reputation to shreds. When he finished, he would leave a highly prejudiced judge.

"I object," Stasson screamed.

"On what grounds?" Kilmore asked softly.

"On the grounds that that remark has nothing to do with the charge. Tillman's trying to besmirch Mr. Kevan's character."

"It seems to me that Mr. Kevan's character is what got him into this mess. Objection overruled."

Jason took off his hat to the prosecutor. He hoped he could stay out of a legal battle with Tillman.

"Shall I repeat the question?" Tillman asked.

"I don't abuse women," Kevan said sullenly.

Tillman's eyebrows rose. "No? What would you call what happened last night? Certainly not affection. You ruined six girls' dresses, and you mauled them until their sheer numbers overcame you." Disgust was in his eyes. "It takes a brave man to go up against women." He shook his head. "That's all, your honor, but may I suggest something?" At Kilmore's nod Tillman said, "If your honor does find Mr. Kevan guilty, and from the evidence we've heard I don't see how there can be any other decision, I believe the cost of the girls' clothing should be added to Mr. Kevan's fine."

Kilmore nodded judiciously. "A sound point, Mr. Tillman."

Stasson was on his feet again, yelling his objection.

"Now what is it, Mr. Stasson?" Kilmore asked in a weary tone.

"I request the judge to ignore Mr. Tillman's last speech. It is highly prejudicial, intended solely to influence the judge."

Judge Kilmore's fierce eyes raked Stasson. "You think I'm incapable of making a decision without being influenced?" he asked softly.

Stasson saw how he had blundered, and he weakly shook his head. "No, your honor. But can't you see how this has gone? Everybody here is determined to get Mr. Kevan, solely because he works for the Rock Island Railroad. How is it going to sound when Mr. Kevan reports that no visitor can expect justice in this town? How will it sound—"

"That's enough, Mr. Stasson," Kilmore snapped.

Stasson still struggled to speak, and Kilmore stabbed a finger at him. "One more word, and I hold you for contempt of court. I warn you the fine will not be small."

That shut Stasson's mouth, and he looked stricken. He sat down beside Kevan, and defeat dripped from him.

"Mr. Kevan," the judge said icily, "approach the bench."

Kevan did so. Kilmore looked intently at the cringing culprit. "This court finds you guilty as charged. You destroyed the peace and created a nuisance. The fine will be one hundred dollars." He glanced at Tillman and grinned wickedly. "I haven't forgotten your suggestion, Mr. Tillman. Do you have a value for the six dresses?"

"I have, sir. The girls value those dresses at forty dollars apiece. It comes to two hundred and forty dollars."

"I can figure," Kilmore said testily. "I'm increasing the fine by two hundred and fifty dollars."

"I haven't got that kind of money with me," Kevan bawled.

"Then I advise you to make arrangements to| get it, for you will be locked up until the total fine is paid."

Kevan was livid. "You'll regret this," he said viciously.

Kilmore leaned forward. "Are you threatening me, Mr. Kevan?"

"You're damned right. You won't forget this day as long as you live."

"That will cost you fifty dollars more for contempt of court," Kilmore snapped.

Kevan was seized up in a wash of rage, and he couldn't be stopped. "Yes, and I'll make the miserable towns of Enid and Pond Creek sorry for this day. I'll do everything I can to crush them."

"That's another fifty dollars, Mr. Kevan. Do you want to keep on? Every word from now on will cost you an additional fifty dollars."

Stasson was at Kevan's side, frantically pulling on his arm. He managed to drag Kevan back to his chair. Kevan looked as though he was going to have a stroke.

"The total is four hundred and fifty dollars, Mr. Kevan," Kilmore pronounced. "It will be paid before I authorize Sheriff Wheeling to release you."

"I haven't got that kind of money on me," Kevan screamed.

"Then you'd better get it, or you'll be held in Enid."

Kevan held his head in his hands. Jason had the impression the man was sobbing. "I can wire my bank to wire authorization to the bank here," he mumbled.

"That will do," Kilmore granted. "Sheriff, take him where he can send the wire. Then take him back to jail and hold him until his answer comes."

Wheeling marched Kevan past where Jason sat, and Jason never saw a man who appeared to be enjoying his work more. Wheeling winked broadly at Jason as he passed.

Kevan looked as though he was going to be sick, and his steps were stumbling.

The six girls surrounded Jason, all chattering with the elation of their victory. "We owe it all to you, Jason," Lily said.

He shook his head. "You owe it to Mr. Tillman and the judge. They saw the justice of your defense. Did you get enough to replace your dresses?"

Lily laughed. "More than enough. When Tillman asked for an estimate, we boosted it. We figured we wouldn't get another crack at our Kevan."

Jason's eyes twinkled. "You earned it." He started to move on, but Ida Belle detained him. She waited until the other girls were gone before she spoke.

"Jason, will I see you again?" She couldn't hide the wistfulness in her voice.

He said it as kindly as he could: "I doubt it, Ida Belle. With my business in Pond Creek—" He paused, at a loss for words.

Ida Belle sighed. "I know. I'm grateful for everything you did."

Jason looked around and noticed that ferret-faced reporter Moore curiously watching them. He decided he had better move on before

Moore tried to exercise his instincts. "I'll see you again, Ida Belle," he said and walked to the door. Right then, he would give long odds that they wouldn't meet again.

He looked back, and Moore had joined Ida Belle. Just seeing them together made Jason uncomfortable. He hoped Ida Belle was discreet in anything she said to the reporter.

"You sure beat that railroad man, Ida Belle," Moore said effusively. "I was glad to see it."

Ida Belle's eyes were fixed on Jason, and her thoughts were elsewhere. "Were you?" she asked absently.

"I sure was," Moore said heartily. "Wasn't that Jason Keeler you were talking to?"

Ida Belle nodded.

"He did you a lot of good in that trial," Moore said.

"Yes, he did," Ida Belle agreed.

"Have you known him long?"

"Almost ever since Enid was established."

Moore's eyes gleamed. There was a story here if he could dig it out. "He sure is a valuable friend," he said. "He put out quite a bit of effort for you with that ride back to Pond Creek last night and back again this morning."

Ida Belle's thoughts were still elsewhere, and she said, "He didn't ride back to Pond Creek."

The gleam burned more brightly in Moore's eyes. "He didn't? Where did he stay?"

"Slim Trevlin rented him a room at the Palace." She frowned at Moore. "Why are you so interested?"

Moore almost whooped with delight. He knew there was a story here. Hell, Ida Belle's words were proof there was more than just friendship between her and Keeler. "I thought with such a friendship between you two, you'd be concerned where he stayed."

Ida Belle realized her mistake. "You're guessing at a lot," she said indignantly.

"Am I?" Moore asked mockingly, backing away from her. He had a story to write.

Ida Belle bit her lip as she watched Moore go. She hoped she hadn't harmed Jason by telling Moore that much. She shook her head in anger. Jason hadn't cautioned her about not talking about what he did, but if it came out in the paper it might hurt him. He had a good woman he was crazy about. It might not set so well with April.

CHAPTER FIVE

Jason was busy for three days after the trial. The controversy with the railroad had done him a lot of good. It had brought him recognition and business. He didn't know how this bitter wrangle would turn out, but it had put Enid and Pond Creek on the map.

The postman ambled into the office. "Not much today, Jason. An official-looking letter from Washington and a copy of the Enid *Wave*. I was in Enid and picked it up. Thought you'd like to see it."

Jason accepted both indifferently. He didn't think either of them would be interesting. Probably another self-explanatory letter from Washington, solving nothing. Washington could spend more time on a matter and accomplish less than anything Jason had ever seen.

He leaned back in his chair, propped his feet up on his desk, and slit open the letter. He scanned the few lines, his eyes growing more unbelieving with each word. "I'll be a—" he exclaimed. Washington had finally acted. The few lines announced that all four towns, North and South Enid and North and South Pond Creek, would be granted post offices. Jason's face clouded. He didn't see where this would do any good; it would just add to the increasing confusion. South Pond Creek wouldn't be any better off. It had a post office now, but its citizens would have to mail their letters from North Pond Creek, as that was the only location of a depot. Their mail would be sent from there, and South Pond Creek citizens would have to make frequent trips to check on their incoming mail. Worse, South Pond Creek still had to go after passengers left at the depot in North Pond Creek. Already, ugliness was beginning to leak out of the situation. Jason had heard of several incidents that happened to South Pond Creek citizens. On going to the depot after passengers left there, their rigs were overturned and harnesses cut. South Pond Creek merchants had to supply armed guards for every trip to pick up freight at the north town. Yesterday, Jason had heard that a stage was supplied to meet the passenger trains. The driver carried a Winchester.

It was an intolerable situation. If it kept on, it wouldn't be long before blood would be shed. Human nature would stand only so much bickering and quarreling before it exploded.

Jason tossed the letter onto his desk. Well, there was nothing he could do about it now. He picked up the copy of the *Wave*. There would be a story in it about the trial.

Jason scanned it rapidly. It was straightforward

reporting until he came to the final two paragraphs. His eyes darkened and his face flushed. Why, that blasted Moore! Jason remembered seeing him talking to Ida Belle. She had obviously told Moore all the facts, but Jason couldn't believe she would turn on him like this:

Ida Belle was fortunate that Jason Keeler came along at the opportune time. He arrived at the height of the brawl and separated the women from the unfortunate John Kevan. All parties were battered and disheveled, but Kevan took the worst of the punishment. One could not help but wonder what would have happened to him if Keeler hadn't happened along. Keeler is an old friend of Ida Belle's. She admitted that she had known him for a long time. In fact, this reporter got the impression that at some past time Keeler had been an ardent swain. Since Keeler didn't return to Pond Creek that night, one cannot help but speculate what his extra reward was for his help. But he broke no laws, and that is not our concern. Kevan was found guilty and fined heavily. That fine included replacing the dresses that were destroyed in the donnybrook. He was unable to pay his fine and was held in the local jail until he heard from his telegram to a Chicago bank. He left after paying his fine, swearing he would never return to Enid again. He also vowed Enid would be sorry it ever arrested him. He made a similar threat in the courtroom. One can't help but speculate what was in Kevan's mind. He works for the Rock Island Railroad. If he has power in his job, this reporter cannot help but wonder how that power will show up. I can only say that both Enid and Pond Creek had better be on the alert.

"You son of a—" Jason roared. Moore had written a skillful story. He had laced his facts with innuendos and guesses that were almost barefaced lies.

Jason crumpled up the paper and flung it from him. He jumped to his feet and paced about the room. That story wouldn't do him any good in any place. He stopped, his face going strained. April! What would she think when she read this story? He groaned hollowly. This was bound to shatter her faith in him. He had to explain this to her as soon as possible.

He picked up the paper and smoothed it out, then added the Washington letter to the small bundle. He had been looking for an excuse the past several days to see April again. Well, he had it now, he thought grimly as he went out the door.

He was riding through Enid's business district when he saw Moore come out of the *Wave*'s office. Jason choked back a curse. He had a few words to exchange with this man. He jumped off, tethered Dandy, and hurried after him. Moore was long-legged, however, and had picked up a quarter-block lead while Jason was tying his horse. Jason was panting when he finally caught up with him.

"Hold up, you," he said jerkily. "I want to talk to you."

Jason's flushed face and fire-flashing eyes alerted Moore. He backed cautiously away. "What's eating on you?"

"Your lying story about the trial."

Moore's eyes gleamed. Where there was so much smoke, there had to be some fire. "Isenberg read my story. He thought it was just fine."

Jason fumed. As editor, Isenberg had the final say about what went into the *Wave*. Satisfying him was all that Moore had to worry about.

"Do you know what this could do to my reputation?" Jason demanded.

Moore grinned. He had Jason on the defensive, and he knew it. "Anything in it that's untrue? You have known Ida Belle for several years. You spent some time with her. It looks as though old ties are hard to break."

Jason wanted to smash his lying face. He half-raised his fist, then lowered it. He had no doubt that he could whip Moore, but what good would it do him? Anybody hearing about the fracas would only be more convinced that what Moore wrote was true.

"Go to hell," Jason stormed. He stabbed a finger at Moore. "Keep this in your solid head: Don't cross me again." He whirled and walked back to his horse. Moore's pleased chuckle was only a further goad.

Jason mounted Dandy and rode to the Budd house. Arnold Budd answered Jason's knock, and he didn't seem too happy to see him.

"Yes, Jason?" Budd asked in a queer, stiff manner.

"Is April here?"

Budd's face froze, and his eyes were evasive. "She is, but maybe it would be best not to see her now. She's pretty upset."

Jason had a queasy, sinking feeling in his stomach. He knew April had already read the last issue of the *Wave*.

"Where is she, Arnold? I'm going to see her."

Budd's sigh was an admission of defeat. "All right. She's in the kitchen. But I think you'll be sorry."

"Maybe," Jason said bleakly and strode toward the kitchen door. He pushed it aside and entered. April was at the stove, her back turned toward him. "April, I want to talk to you."

She whirled, her face flaming, her mouth a thin line. In her temper, she didn't look like the same April. "I don't want to talk to you," she snapped. "I didn't think you'd have the gall to show your face here after what you did."

Jason groaned. He still carried a copy of the newspaper, and she stared at it. "Aw, April," he protested. "That was only a figment of a reporter's imagination. Aren't you going to listen to me?"

"No," she said stubbornly, then reconsidered. "All right. I'd like to hear you try to lie your way out of this."

Jason thought frantically. What was he going to say to get out of this mess?

"Do you deny knowing this Ida Belle?" she threw at him.

He shook his head. "I wouldn't try to do that. I met her shortly after I arrived in Oklahoma. She was friendly—"

Her snort of disdain interrupted him. "I'll bet she was."

Jason ignored that. "And I was a young and lonely man."

April rocked her head back and forth in distress. "Then you don't deny anything?"

"Why should I?" he asked levelly. "All that happened before I met you. Since I looked at you, I haven't had room in my thoughts for any other woman."

For a moment, he thought she was softening; then she recoiled from him as though she was afraid he was going to try to touch her. "More lies," she said shrilly. "After the fight, you spent the night with her, didn't you?"

Jason flinched at the accusation. "I didn't, April. I stayed at the Palace, but not with her. It saved me a trip back to Pond Creek. I had to be back in Enid to be at the trial the following morning. That damned reporter suggested I might have spent the night with Ida Belle. He built up this whole damned story."

April's eyes were squinched tight so she wouldn't have to look at him. "You pulled this Ida Belle out of trouble. Didn't she think of an extra reward?"

"Stop it," Jason said harshly. "You don't know what you're talking about." He walked to her and seized her upper arms. He had to shake some sense into her. "Believe me, April, it's not like you think at all. After I met you, I closed the book on that chapter of my life. From then on, you were the only woman who existed for me."

Oh, if she would only look at him. Perhaps she would see that he wasn't lying to her.

She flung his hands from her arms, and her eyes were wide open, blazing at him. "Liar, liar." She was very close to hysterics. She closed her eyes again, and tears slowly leaked out of them. "Get out of here," she sobbed. "I never want to look at you again."

He thought his heart was dying as he backed out of the room. When a woman made up her mind to do something as drastic as April had, there was no chance of reasoning with her.

Arnold was waiting for him, and he looked anxious. "How did it go, Jason?"

"Rotten. I couldn't even get her to listen to me."

"I was afraid of that," Arnold said gloomily. "Give it a little time, and—"

"No," Jason said flatly. He had been cruelly lacerated, and it would take a long time for the hurt to ease. If she didn't want to see him, he wasn't going to press it. Then he remembered the Washington letter. He handed it to Budd. "Maybe this will brighten you up."

Budd scanned the letter, then looked up at Jason. "What does it mean?"

"It means that all four towns will have a post office. Maybe that's the beginning of straightening out this mess."

"What good will that do, if the railroad only stops at their depots?"

"That remains to be seen. At least Washington is aware of what's happening here. Maybe they'll discover enough backbone to issue orders to the Rock Island."

He started for the door, and Budd said, "I'm sorry, Jason."

Jason gave him a twisted grimace. "Not half as sorry as I am." He gently closed the door behind him, but he wanted to slam it. Halfway down the walk he looked back at the house. A lot of his dreams had died in there.

He mounted and headed straight out of town. The sooner he left, the more satisfied he would be. Right now he could honestly say he would never return to Enid.

The most direct course out of town led through the business district. Up ahead, Ida Belle was coming out of a store with four other girls. Jason's wrath bubbled up. If she hadn't given that interview to Moore, none of this would have happened.

He edged over to where the five women were walking and called out in a choked voice, "Ida Belle. I want to talk to you."

She looked up, startled at his voice, and left the group. "You look mad about something, Jason," she commented.

"I'm damned mad," he said from between gritted teeth. "Why did you give that interview to Moore?"

She looked at him with widening eyes. "I just answered his questions. I couldn't see where they could do any harm. I didn't lie."

Jason barely managed to keep his anger under control. He wanted to shake her, but that wouldn't change anything. "No harm?" he groaned. "It only wrecked all my future hopes with April. What do you think she thought when she read that miserable account?"

Ida Belle sucked in a breath, and her eyes were remorseful. "You know I didn't want to cause you any trouble, Jason. I didn't read the story. Lily read it and told me what it said. She didn't think it was that bad."

"Bad?" Jason raged. "That story made it sound as though I spent all my time with you. What would April think when she read that?"

Ida Belle's eyes crinkled up with distress. "I didn't say anything like that, Jason. I said I knew you, that in the past you came into the saloon. That's all."

"All?" he howled. "I've never seen April so furious. She never wants to see me again."

"No," Ida Belle said in distress. "You didn't come near me after the fight."

"That's not the way Moore wrote it. He made it sound as though I received an extra reward from you. Maybe not in so many words, but his meaning was clear."

"That's not fair," she objected. "Both of us know it wasn't like that."

"But April doesn't know it," he growled. "I'll never forgive you for this, Ida Belle."

He whirled and walked back to Dandy. He rode away without looking back.

No, Jason, Ida Belle thought. It wasn't like that at all. She hadn't intended it to turn out this way, but she had done a grievous hurt to an old friend. She had to do something about straightening out this mess.

Her face hardened with determination. It might be difficult to talk to April Budd, for she knew what the so-called decent class of people thought about saloon girls. But April's going to listen to me, Ida Belle thought. It's the least I can do for Jason.

CHAPTER SIX

Kevan chewed nervously on his lower lip as he approached the woman sitting outside his father-in-law's door. Mrs. Templeton was a prim-looking woman who had been Mr. Cable's secretary for longer than Kevan could remember. Frankly, he was a little frightened of her.

"Good morning, Mrs. Templeton," he said fawning. "Is Dad in this morning?"

She stared at him wide-eyed, almost to the point of horror. He had changed clothing—his linen was faultless—but he couldn't do anything about his face. The bruises and scratches from the fight in Enid were glowing in all their glory of discoloration.

"What happened to you?" she gasped.

Kevan dismissed her question with a wave of his hand. He had no intention of going into details about the fight, particularly with her. "Nothing important," he said easily. "May I go in to see Dad?"

"Of course, John," she said, simpering. This man was only a vice-president of the railroad, but one of these days he would step into President Cable's shoes. A less important employee never made the mistake of overlooking where the future power lay.

Kevan paused before the big door, adjusted his lapels, and straightened his tie. How he dreaded this coming session. Ransom Cable was his father-in-law, and John's position was due solely to his marriage to Mary Ann, Cable's daughter. Cable was completely wrapped up in his only daughter, and he had created the job for Kevan. He winced as he thought of how Cable would look if he knew the exact details of that fight. He drew a deep breath. Cable must never know. It wasn't very likely that he would, however, for that small town of Enid was a long distance away. What happened there would never reach the attention of a busy railroad president.

He rapped softly on the door, and heard Cable's muted voice, "Come in." Kevan frowned. Cable sounded a little irritable this morning. He often was, for many details picked at him.

Kevan opened the door of the ornate office and crossed the soft thick carpet. He had been in here many times, and every time, he was impressed with its luxury. If things worked out as they should, all this would be his one of these days.

He stopped before the desk and cleared his throat. "Hello, Dad," he said. His voice was always in a higher range whenever he faced this great man.

Cable was studying some figures, and he didn't

look up immediately. "I thought you'd be back before now, John. Mary Ann was beginning to worry."

"Something came up," Kevan said, steadying his voice. He managed to make his laugh rueful. "Something I had no control over."

Cable looked up then, and his eyes sharpened. "My God, John. You look like you've been in a fight."

Kevan laughed again. He had had no trouble convincing Mary Ann that the fight was not his fault. It might be a little more difficult with Cable, however, for he had a sharp and perceptive mind. "I'm afraid it wasn't much of a fight, sir. I didn't put up much of a showing. Six of Enid's toughs jumped me. They worked me over pretty thoroughly."

That famed Cable dander was rising, for his face clouded. "Couldn't you call on the law for assistance?"

Kevan laughed wryly. "That was the worst part of it, sir. I did ask the sheriff for help. He arrested me. I was held in jail overnight for disturbing the peace."

His temper now in full sway, Cable banged his desk with a heavy fist. How he wished Mary Ann had fallen in love with more of a man, but that couldn't be altered now. She was in love with John Kevan, the kind of a love that wouldn't listen to advice or direction. The marriage was only two years old. It would take more time to open her eyes.

Cable was breathing heavily as he sank into his chair. He studied the marks on Kevan's face. "It looks like they used their nails instead of their fists."

"They were maniacs, sir," Kevan said. "They tore at me like animals. I couldn't stand them off. I was lucky the sheriff happened along. I thought it was help coming." His face twisted. "He arrested me. I had to stand trial in their local court. The judge was completely unreasonable. When I tried to explain, he kept raising the fine. He wound up by fining me four hundred and fifty dollars."

Cable was having difficulty with his breathing, and his face was flushed. "Oh, those yokels!" he exploded. "Why do you think they made the fine so heavy?"

Kevan shrugged. "The only reason I can think of is they found out I'm a Rock Island man. You know how troublesome Enid and Pond Creek have been lately."

Cable's nostrils flared. "I'll give them better reason to scream," he said. "I'll make it so tough for them, they'll be hunting holes to crawl in. Did you get any names of those toughs?"

"Just one," Kevan answered. "A Jason Keeler from Pond Creek. He happened to come along and join in." He kept his face impassive, though he seethed inside. God, how he hated Keeler. If he could only find some way to get even—

"I've got some influence in Washington," Cable said. "I'll use it to make Enid and Pond Creek sorry they ever existed." He stopped, his eyes going wide with a sharp calculation. "John, how would you like to be in charge of the affairs of those two towns? After what they did to you, I know you're aching to repay their insults."

Kevan breathed in sudden elation. He would like nothing better, with the power of the Rock Island behind him and what power of the government Cable could muster. There would never be a better opportunity to even the slate.

"I'd like it, sir," he said huskily. "I've thought about the indignity I suffered until I can't get it out of my mind. Mary Ann will be pleased, too. She's been worried about me." He paused in reflection. "How far shall I go, sir, in retaliation?"

"As far as you think necessary," Cable barked. "If the Rock Island isn't powerful enough to whip two miserable towns, I think the might of the government will change their minds. Don't be too concerned about legalities. If Enid and Pond Creek want violence, they'll get it."

He got up, came around the desk, and draped an arm about Kevan's shoulders. "If there's anything you need, just ask for it. I'm expecting you to win this fight."

Kevan's eyes gleamed. "I'll win it, sir. You can

count on it." Elation bubbled up within him. He had vowed in Enid's courtroom that he would make Enid and Pond Creek sorry. At the time, they were only empty words. Now they had raw meaning.

Ida Belle hesitated outside the Budd door. She knew very well what her reception could be. Was she prepared to face insults? She sighed, raised her knuckles, and rapped vigorously on the door. She knew what she could be facing when she came here.

Arnold Budd's eyes went round in shock as he opened the door and looked at the caller.

"I want to talk to Miss April," Ida Belle said sharply. "Don't make up your mind. You don't even know who I am."

"I know you," Budd said stiffly. "I've seen you about town. You were pointed out to me."

Ida Belle smiled bleakly. Here was one of those decent people, a person who had only icy contempt for a saloon girl.

"Yes," she acknowledged. "I'm Ida Belle. Will you please tell April that I'm here? She won't regret talking to me. It's most important."

Budd looked doubtfully at her. "I doubt if she will talk to you. I'm sure she doesn't want to—"

He broke off before Ida Belle's level, candid eyes. "Have any contact with me," she finished for him. "Tell her what I just said. I think she'll be the sorriest woman in the world if she doesn't talk to me."

Budd shook his head. "I'll try. But I doubt it'll do any good. I wouldn't attempt to force her."

"Just try," Ida Belle urged. She stood outside the door. Budd hadn't even asked her in. Her face was a hard mask as she waited. Through the years she had gotten used to this kind of treatment.

Budd came back in a moment, and he was shaking his head more vigorously. "I was right," he said in small triumph. "April doesn't have any desire to talk to you. She says she will not talk to you at any time or any place."

Ida Belle's eyes glinted as she nodded. That was what April thought. She will talk to me, and I'll pick the time and place. How had Jason come to think he couldn't live without such a stiff-necked woman?

Ida Belle carried her head high as she went down the walk. She didn't look back, but she'd bet Budd was watching her. Yes, and she imagined April was peeking out of one of the windows.

Two days later, she followed April into the shopping district and saw her enter Lord's General Store. This was the time and place she had been seeking.

Ida Belle marched into the store, and her steps were firm. April was looking over some dress material; Ida Belle stopped beside her. April barely glanced at her at first, then she inhaled deeply in outrage. Her face was stiff, and she started to move away.

"Ah, you know me," Ida Belle said in a satisfied tone.

"As well as I want to," April said coldly. Ida Belle had moved to block her passage. "Will you please get out of my way?" she demanded.

"Not unless you listen to what I have to say." Ida Belle had faced indignant females before; April's expression didn't faze her. "If you try to walk away without listening to me, I'll make a scene you'll never forget. It'll be the talk of the town for months to come."

April glanced hastily about the store. A half-dozen other women were there. So far, the confrontation had aroused no attention. But it would, if Ida Belle carried out her threat.

April's indecision was visible. How she detested this woman! "Go ahead," she said ungraciously. "Say what you have to say."

"I suppose you read that story in the *Wave*?"

April nodded unwillingly.

"You are a very foolish woman," Ida Belle murmured, "to believe a story some reporter writes instead of the man who loves you."

April's voice raised. "Do you deny being on friendly terms with Jason?" She put a lot of contempt in the name.

"I knew Jason when he first came to Enid. He was young and lonely."

April paled. "That relationship didn't break off. Try and deny that."

"He was passing by and saw the fight with Kevan. He stopped to see if he could assist us."

"And stopped to spend the night with you as a special reward."

Ida Belle sighed. How difficult it was to talk to a so-called decent woman. They had unshakable minds formed by preconceived ideas and their rigid upbringing. "After the fight, he said he was going to stop in a hotel. He wanted to save him-self the trip back to Pond Creek and the ride back here in the morning, since he had to be at the trial as an important witness. I told him he'd be more comfortable in a room at the Palace. That's as far as it went."

Ida Belle shook her head as April's expression didn't change. "You could be a lucky woman, April. Maybe one of these days you'll realize that. I can't say any more." She turned and walked out of the door.

April remained where she was. Was Ida Belle telling the truth? Everything began to sound so plausible. She turned away from the table of dress material and left Lord's, her face troubled. Ida Belle could be doing her a favor.

CHAPTER SEVEN

Jason carved open another letter from Washington. His correspondence with the government had increased considerably. At least they were aware of what was going on.

The Rock Island still ignored the two south towns, stopping only at the depots, roaring on past South Enid and South Pond Creek without even a pretense of stopping. The government was aware of that, but so far they had done nothing about it.

Jason read the letter with interest. "Be informed," the letter read, "that the Rock Island Railroad has been ordered to leave mail at both South Enid and South Pond Creek. Any violation of this order will bring dire consequences."

Jason's expression didn't lighten. He didn't know how much good that would do. All he could do was wait and see how things worked out. Sometimes he wondered if he had been wise to get into this fight of town against railroad. He couldn't say he didn't enjoy it, but it took a lot of his time; he had his own work to take care of. Unofficially, he had been appointed to head the town's fight, and hardly an hour passed without another townsman wandering in seeking fresh information on how they stood against the

Rock Island. Jason's knowledge of profanity had increased. He didn't doubt that he had heard every obscene word in existence.

"Jason."

His name was so softly spoken that he wasn't sure he had heard it. He slowly turned in his chair, and his heart bounded up into his throat and lodged there. "April," he cried, and leaped to his feet. After the last time he had tried to talk to her, he thought he would never see her again, at least not here.

Her face was pale but composed, and she looked directly at him. God, her loveliness was so great it put a physical ache in him.

"I didn't know whether or not you'd want to talk to me again," she murmured.

He advanced toward her, his eyes locked on hers. "What put that foolish notion in your head?"

She was suffering; it was in her face, but her eyes still hadn't wavered. "The way I acted," she said steadily. "I wouldn't blame you if you never spoke to me again."

Something drastic had occurred to change her so completely.

"What happened, April?" he asked gently.

"Ida Belle came to see me. I wouldn't see her, but she was determined. She waited until she caught me in Lord's store and hemmed me in. She promised me a terrible scene if I didn't listen to her."

Jason's lips twitched, but he managed to keep the grin hidden. "Ida Belle's got a lot of determination," he said gravely.

She nodded agreement. "She told me pretty much what you tried to tell me. She said the time you knew her happened when you first came to Enid, before we met. I realized that what a man or woman did before they met the one they wanted doesn't count. I spent some miserable hours thinking about that."

Jason beamed. So Ida Belle had come to his aid. Bless her tough little heart. "Was that all she said?"

"I guess she hadn't seen you until the night of the fight with the railroad man. She said you happened to ride by and stopped to help the women." Her laugh was shaky. "I heard the girls could have whipped him, but they were grateful to you."

Jason nodded. "They had him whipped when I arrived. Did she tell you where I spent the night?"

April nodded jerkily. "She said at the Palace— in a separate room. It saved you the trip of coming back to Enid. She said if I didn't straighten things out with you, I wasn't as smart as she thought I was."

Jason spread his arms, and April came into them. She looked up at him. "I didn't want anybody to consider me stupid."

"April," he said huskily, and held her tight. He kissed her long and hard, and there wasn't a flaw in her response.

"Will you ever forgive me, Jason?"

"I don't know what you're talking about," he replied.

"Oh, Jason," she said, and raised her head again.

"I'm going to ride back to Enid with you, April."

"You don't have to," she objected. "You don't have to prove anything to me."

"But it's necessary," Jason said calmly. "I've got another letter from Washington to show Arnold." He smiled impishly. "By the way Washington is firing off letters to me it looks as though I'll have to come over to your house often."

She snugged his arm to her side. "Nothing would suit me better, Jason. If I get impatient, all I have to do is think of those dreary days when I was positive I wouldn't see you again."

He was whistling happily as he and April went out of the door. It might be a long time before he saw Ida Belle again and could properly thank her. He would be wise not to stop at the saloon again. No, he would wait until everything cooled down.

He helped April into her saddle and whistled all the way back to Enid.

Budd showed a brief period of shock when he

saw them together, but he recovered quickly. He beamed like a full harvest moon. "I can't tell you how happy I am to see you two have settled your quarrel."

"It was all my fault, Papa," April said. "I jumped to conclusions when there were none."

Jason placed an arm about her shoulders. "I don't think anyone could blame you for feeling like you did."

April ran her fingertips down his cheek. "Still trying to make it easy for my stupidity. I'll get some lunch ready."

Jason shook his head as she left the room. "That's some girl, Arnold."

"Don't I know it. I was afraid you two would separate forever."

"It could have happened," Jason said gravely. He debated telling Budd that Ida Belle was the one responsible for bringing them back together, but decided against it. It was best to leave that subject undiscussed. Instead he handed Budd the last letter from Washington. "Looks like we're winning our battle against the railroad." He couldn't keep the triumph out of his voice.

"You think this is going to make that lousy railroad do what's right?"

"They'd better," Jason replied. "Or they'll be facing those dire consequences mentioned in the letter."

Budd snorted. "That won't stop them. I noticed

they were building something against their track when I passed by there a few hours ago."

"What was it?" Jason asked, his curiosity stirred.

Budd frowned. "I couldn't make it out. Looked like some kind of a crane, a metal upright higher than a railroad car. It had an arm extending| from it over the track. What's wrong?" he asked in alarm at Jason's blackening face.

"I know what that's going to be," Jason complained. "I've seen them before."

"What is it?"

"You named it right. It's a crane. Outgoing mail can be hung on it. The train will pick it up and leave incoming mail without even slowing down."

"Will it work, Jason?"

Jason muttered a soft oath. "Sometimes it does. Other times it doesn't. I've seen mail scattered all over hell when the connection was missed."

"Will that satisfy Washington?"

"It might, if they don't get many complaints. Let's go down and take a look at it."

April came out of the kitchen and began setting the table. "Lunch will be ready in a few minutes."

Budd shook his head. "We won't be here, April."

She placed her hands on her hips. "Why not?"

"Got to go down and see something the railroad's installing. It'll be vital to the town."

"You, too?" April asked Jason.

He nodded soberly. "Afraid so, April."

"How long is this going to go on?" she asked indignantly.

"Until we whip that crummy railroad," Jason said soberly. He placed a light kiss on her forehead. "We'll be back just as soon as we can."

Her face showed she wasn't happy when he left the house.

A small crowd had gathered to watch the railroad employees put the final touches on the job they were working on. The upright was thoroughly anchored, and the arm extending almost to the tracks was just being attached.

"What's that thing supposed to be?" Budd demanded.

One of the workmen winked at the others. "The townies are already beginning to complain. They don't appreciate anything the Rock Island does for them."

Budd was ready to explode, and Jason laid a restraining hand on his arm. "We'll wait until we see how this contrivance works before we howl."

Both of them were back when the afternoon train was scheduled. "Train's coming," Budd announced.

Jason nodded. He didn't need to see the train. He could hear the clackety-clack of the wheels. Now they would see how this contraption worked.

"Ain't that train coming awfully fast?" Budd asked.

"About the same as usual," Jason responded. He wondered if the engineer would slow down as he approached the crane.

Jason saw the mail clerk standing in the opened door of the express car, trying to hook the mail pouch on the hook supplied for that purpose. It might be fine, if it worked. But the man missed the hook, and the mail pouch fell to the railroad right-of-way and bounced along.

Budd raved as he watched the pouch split open and scatter its contents. Letters and small packages were strewn everywhere. The mail clerk added insult to injury by waving at Budd and Jason as the car passed them.

"If this ain't a damned mess," Budd stormed.

A light breeze began to scatter the letters. Jason saw several of them move a few feet before they settled down again.

"We better pick them up," he said angrily, "before they're blown over the entire county."

The two men went slowly down the track, stopping every now and then to bend and retrieve a piece of mail. The sun was hot, and it didn't take much of this exertion to break out sweat on their faces.

The wind strengthened, picking up the letters with greater alacrity. In chasing one letter, Budd tripped over a rail and fell. His trouser knee split open against the small rocks cushioning the ties and rails. He struggled to his feet, furious. Blood seeped from the lacerated knee.

"Those bastards," he screamed. "I wish I had a gun. I'd shoot every one of the men who constructed this thing."

Jason wanted to smirk at the perfect picture of wrath. "Don't blame them," he counseled. "Blame the officials of the railroad. They issued the orders."

Budd's wrath left his face, leaving it despairing and sunken. "What are we going to do, Jason?"

"Finish picking up this mail, then take it in to Isenberg's office. His screams of outrage can reach a lot more people than we can."

They finished picking up the scattered mail, then spent another ten minutes to be sure they hadn't overlooked any.

"I guess that's all," Jason announced. "If you think this makes you mad, wait until you hear Isenberg. He loves this town."

Isenberg looked up from his cluttered desk. He was a huge man with a paunch that overflowed his chair. Ordinarily he was good-humored, but also quick to anger.

"Oddest-looking mailmen I've ever seen," he observed as he noticed their burdened arms.

"You wouldn't think so if you saw the way the Rock Island left this mail," Budd growled. "Jason and I had to pick up this mail off the right-of-way."

Isenberg's face was beginning to stiffen. "What happened? That new contraption didn't work?"

"It didn't come close," Jason replied. "You should have been down there to see it." He described the pouch missing the hook and ripping open. "Mail scattered all over. We think we got it all."

Isenberg was beginning to fire. "Did the train stop at the north addition?" he questioned.

"You know it," Jason replied. "That's where the railroad depot is, isn't it?"

Isenberg blew out a gusty breath. "Something's got to be done about this. We can't let the Rock Island continue to get away with this kind of handling." He reached for a piece of paper and a pencil.

"We hoped you would react like this," Jason said with satisfaction. "You can arouse a lot more people than we could."

Isenberg scribbled for several moments, then leaned back in his chair and read what he had written: "It is time for the good citizens to do something about the high-handed way the Rock Island is treating them. There is only one Enid, the portion now called South Enid. But does the railroad stop here? It does not. It does not even slow down. At the government's orders to deliver mail to South Enid, the railroad has constructed a contraption on which to leave the mail. I call the device the Snubbing Post for no better term to describe it. Today, the railroad missed the hook on which they were supposed to leave the mail pouch. The pouch fell to the ground and ripped open, scattering mail all over. If it wasn't for the efforts of Arnold Budd and Jason Keeler, I'm afraid most of that mail would have been lost. How long will the citizens of Enid put up with this kind of treatment? The north addition, which the railroad has backed, has a regular depot. I call the north addition the Tank. The train stops at the depot. The Tank got its mail in decent order. There is only one Enid. The post office address is simply Enid. The post office in the addition is called North Enid."

He stopped reading and looked at Jason and Budd. "What do you think?"

"Couldn't be better," Budd approved.

Jason looked dubious. "I know how you feel, but it just occurred to me that we might be playing into the railroad's hands. Won't this be setting the north towns against the south towns even more?"

Isenberg thrust a belligerent chin toward Jason. "Who cares if it does? Do you think we should take all the crap the railroad is handing us lying down?"

"No," Jason said thoughtfully. "But I don't approve of urging a war on the settlers." He shrugged, then said, "Go ahead and publish your story."

"I intend to," Isenberg said brusquely.

"Maybe some good will come out of it," Jason said mildly. "Hold a copy for me. I'll see that Washington gets it. Maybe it'll make them realize what we're up against."

Jason walked to the door with Budd, then turned. "When will that copy be ready?"

"The next edition won't be out for a couple of days," the editor growled.

Jason nodded. "I'll be by to pick it up."

Outside he said, "Arnold, it's always the same. The men the least capable of fighting are the most belligerent. They're happy to stand by and encourage everybody else to do the fighting."

"I didn't think his story was that bad," Budd objected.

"It was written well enough," Jason conceded. "We'd better ride over to Pond Creek and see if they've had the same trouble."

"Hadn't we better stop by and tell April what happened to us?"

"You can tell her when you get home tonight. Right now, I've got the feeling we've got more urgent things to look into."

A crowd had gathered in Pond Creek's main street, and they were in an ugly mood. Every man tried to talk at once, and Jason raised his hands to quiet them. "Easy," he said, nodding at Sam Turner. "Tell me what happened, Sam." Turner was a crusty old character, never hesitating to say what was on his mind. Several times Jason had heard him offend people, and Turner's old age was the only thing that saved him.

Turner was so angry at first that he couldn't talk.

"I can't understand a word you're saying," Jason said. "Take it slower, Sam."

Turner slowed down, but he still spit out his words. "The damned railroad roared through here without even slowing. The mail clerk tried to use that infernal device the railroad put in." He spit savagely.

"And the clerk missed the hook," Jason guessed.

Turner scowled. "He sure as hell did. The pouch broke open and scattered the mail everywhere."

"Were you expecting a letter, Sam?"

"Not me," Turner snorted. "But my wife was. For the past week, she's been expecting a letter from our granddaughter."

Jason shook his head sympathetically. "And the letter was lost?"

Turner uttered a fierce expletive. "Might have been better if it was. No, the letter wasn't lost, but a breeze blew it under the hoofs of a passing mule team. Amy could hardly make out a word that letter said."

It wasn't funny, but Jason almost choked on laughter. "I'm really sorry, Sam."

"That don't do no good," Turner said. "I think it's about time somebody did something about that railroad. We've got to show them we're people and not cattle to drive to market. By God, we're going to do it. Before we get through, that damned Rock Island will treat us with more respect."

Jason's eyes sharpened. In a way, this old man was more dangerous than Isenberg. Isenberg would be content to stay on the sidelines and howl his protests. Turner would not only be in the action, he would likely lead it.

"What are you planning, Sam?"

For a moment, Jason thought Turner was going to tell him, then the old man's lips clamped together. "No," he said violently. "You might try to stop us. I know you're a law-abiding man, but we can't allow you to stop what we've planned. Come down about this time tomorrow if you want to see what's going to come off."

Jason took Budd's arm and led him away. There was no use in further talk with Turner. The only way to find out was to come back the next day.

"What do you think he's planning, Jason?"

"God only knows. That bunch he had with him—" Jason shook his head. "We'll be back tomorrow to find out."

CHAPTER EIGHT

Jason heard the queer noise before he turned the corner. He couldn't make out what it was at first; all he could hear was a heavy, groaning sound and the squealing of overburdened wheels.

He quickened his pace, forcing Budd to break into a trot to keep up. "What is it, Jason?" Budd panted.

Jason hadn't the slightest idea. "We'll find out soon."

He stopped as soon as he rounded the corner. His eyes widened in amazement. This was the damnedest sight he had ever seen. In some way Sam's bunch had propped up a small, ramshackle house and gotten wheels under it. Four stout mules were trying to pull it forward, urged on by stinging whips. With each forward movement, Jason thought the house would fall apart. It swayed and groaned, and its momentum stopped every few feet. Each time it looked as though the house was lodged and nothing could start it again. The mules got additional punishment and the men pushing behind the house strained even harder, trying to find that little bit of power to start the house moving again.

Jason hurried forward and caught up with the house on its next brief stop. "Sam, what do you think you're doing?"

Turner turned, his malicious old eyes filled with triumph. "We're going to put this house across the Rock Island track. That damned train will stop today."

Jason caught his arm. "Who thought of this?"

"I did," Turner said proudly. "We're tired of being walked on. Get out of the way, Jason."

Jason looked at the determined faces of the men with Turner. He couldn't stop them either physically or legally; they would swarm over him if he tried. Reluctantly, he stepped back. Another few dozen yards and the house would be moved onto the tracks.

Jason made one last entreaty. "Sam," he begged, "think of what you're doing. You're destroying property."

"This house?" Turner scoffed. "It was abandoned. Nobody wanted it any more. Hell, it's ready to fall apart."

"I'm not thinking of the house," Jason protested. "I'm thinking of the railroad property. You could wreck the train. The railroad will use all of its power to come down on you. Do you want to go to jail?"

Turner was unperturbed. "Won't be our fault if there's any damage. We're sending a man up the track to flag the train down. If the engineer refuses to heed our warning, that's his business."

Jason gave up. Turner had gone too far to be stopped now. He stepped back and joined Budd, telling him what would happen. Budd said admiringly, "Can't say I blame them. They'll stop that train."

Jason looked dubiously at the ramshackle house. "Maybe not," he grunted.

Men were busy knocking the wheels from under the structure. Finally, it settled down across the track.

By Turner's calculations, the train was due. He picked up a piece of red cloth nailed to a long stick and handed it to a man, then turned him and shoved him down the track. The man ran northward, waving the improvised flag.

Jason couldn't keep his interest from being stirred. "We'll find out in a few minutes whether or not Turner has an idea." He really didn't blame Turner. This wasn't actual violence, but it was close. It would be interesting to see how the railroad reacted.

Soon they could hear the train coming. The flag carrier was still in view. He ran down the track vigorously waving his makeshift flag. If the engineer heeded the warning, there was still time to stop the train.

The train came into view, and the engineer opened his throttle wide. He kept blowing shrill blasts as his own warning for the man to get off the track. Jason sucked in his breath. The flag-man was cutting it close, maybe too close. He kept waving that flag until the train was almost upon him, then he dived wildly to one side. He lit on one shoulder and rolled. The passing train cut him off from Jason's view.

The engineer must have been holding the whistle cord down, for he blew one blast after another. Jason shook his head. Either the engineer was foolhardy or had extraordinary courage.

The engine roared into the house across the track. The house flew apart as though an explosion had demolished it. Boards flew in every direction. The derisive whistle kept blowing as the train roared on.

Turner was so angry he jumped up and down in one spot. "Why, damn him," he panted. "I'll show him he can't do this to us." He looked around for confirmation, and angry men nodded in agreement.

"I'd give it up, Sam," Jason said gently. "It looks as though the railroad is determined not to stop here. There's nothing we can do ourselves to change things."

"The hell there ain't," Turner screamed. "You come back tomorrow, and you'll see."

"It looks like he's really made up his mind," Budd observed as they walked away.

"I still think he's making a mistake," Jason growled.

Jason whistled as he saw what Turner had prepared for the next train. Three heavy freight wagons had been pushed onto the track, the brakes set and locked. To make the obstacle more formidable, the three wagons were chained together.

"Now what do you think?" Turner challenged.

"It won't work any better, Sam. You don't realize the force you're up against."

"You wait and see," Turner snapped.

"That's what I'm going to do."

Turner sent another flagman down the track as he heard the train in the distance. The flagman had learned from yesterday's near-disaster and ran outside of the track. If the engineer insisted on maintaining his speed, there wouldn't be so far to dive to safety. He began waving vigorously before the train came into Jason's view. He never stopped waving as he edged farther from the track.

Either this engineer was fanatically loyal to the Rock Island, or had orders he was afraid to disobey. He opened the throttle to its fullest, and the whistle never stopped its infernal shrieking.

Jason noticed that everybody's mouth was sagging open as the engine drew closer and closer to the freight wagons. Everyone squirmed with the tenseness of anticipation.

The first wagon disintegrated under the impact of the crash, and the air was literally filled with flying debris. That lasted only a fraction of a second, for the engine was then tearing into the second wagon, which had been dragged partially off the track. It didn't matter, however, as the engine hit enough of the second wagon to tear it apart. In another instant, the final wagon was being shredded. Jason wasn't sure, but he thought the engineer thumbed his nose as the train roared out of sight.

The crowd looked bemused, though they were actually stunned.

Jason walked over to Turner. "Satisfied now? All you succeeded in doing was smashing up three good wagons."

He thought Turner would choke on his anger. "Did you see that bastard?" he raved, raising his clenched fists and shaking them in the air. "He thumbed his nose as he went by."

"I guess he earned the right," Jason said wryly. "He sure won today."

Turner glared at Jason, and the pupils of his eyes shrank into blazing pinpoints. "You're the one who told us to wait until the railroad gave us our rights. When the going gets a little tough, you tuck your tail between your legs and run."

Jason spun on his heel. He couldn't take any more of Sam's abuse. "You coming, Arnold?" he threw back over his shoulder.

Budd was undecided. He looked to Turner, then back to Keeler. He sighed heavily and quickened his step to catch up with Jason.

Jason was still seething as he walked into his office. He sat down, put his feet up on the desk, and stared at the far wall.

He was silent for so long that Budd asked uneasily, "What are you thinking about, Jason?"

"What Sam said," Jason replied.

"He's an old man. He could be wrong."

"And he could be right," Jason snapped. "I put down Isenberg for writing that story and staying on the sidelines. Turner and that bunch were trying to do something about this situation."

"They didn't get very far," Budd observed.

"Maybe because they were using the wrong methods," Jason said, his eyes narrowed.

That irritated Budd. "All you're doing is criticizing them. Do you think you could do any better?"

"I could sure get better results," Jason said, unruffled. He jumped to his feet. "I wonder where we could find Sam and that bunch?"

Budd shook his head. "I'm not familiar with Pond Creek."

Jason snapped his fingers. "Probably at Murphy's saloon. Are you coming with me?"

"I wouldn't miss this for the world," Budd replied.

There was loud swearing and arguing coming

from the saloon as they approached it. Then somebody saw them coming through the door, and his hissing quieted all the others. Heads swung toward Jason and Budd, and Jason couldn't find a friendly eye in the room.

"Who asked for you?" Turner growled. "We heard enough of your advice to last us the rest of the month." With each word his ire rose. He jumped to his feet, quivering with indignation. "Who was the first one to encourage us to take a stand against the Rock Island? You!" he bellowed. "But when things look like they could get rough, who's the first one to back out? You know the answer to that!" He sat down, keeping his back defiantly turned toward Jason.

Jason advanced slowly toward his table. "You've been right all along, Sam. The railroad's not going to do the fair thing unless we keep a solid front against them. Things will probably get worse. If we show weakness, the railroad will stir up North Enid and North Pond Creek to move against us. We sure don't want a civil war on our hands."

The stern lines in Turner's face began to soften. "You gonna show us how to do things right?"

"That's why I'm here, Sam," Jason said gently. He looked around at the listening men and saw Cummings, the hardware store owner. "Ben, it's going to be a moonless night. We couldn't find a better time. Have you got any sledgehammers in your store?"

"A new shipment just came in," Cummings replied eagerly. "I've got a dozen. Maybe one or two more."

Jason chuckled. "That oughta do."

"What have you got in mind, Jason?" Turner begged.

"Meet me at the railroad track at midnight," Jason replied. "You won't be disappointed."

It was indeed a dark night, and there wasn't much talk. Almost two hundred men were busy at the tracks. Now and then, there was a muttered curse as a man barked a shin or strained a muscle. The ring of sledges against steel was a constant sound.

Turner paused to mop his sweating face. "Great idea, Jason. By God, that engineer won't roar through here so high and mighty again."

"This is highly illegal, Sam," Jason said gravely. "The Rock Island has a powerful battery of lawyers. Bet on it that they'll be busy laying every charge they can find against us. We could all be facing some jail sentences."

Turner stubbornly shook his head. "Don't care much, Jason. Just once, I'd like to come out ahead. Just once, I'd like to be positive that the train won't roar through Pond Creek."

Jason flexed his hands. They were beginning to

get sore; before long, blisters would be forming. But he felt good. He was no longer an outcast. He was one of them. This was the same sense of belonging that had made him feel so good at the start. Speaking out against the railroad had given him standing and pumped life into his struggling business. He didn't give a damn if this *was* illegal. He'd consider it only as a blow struck in self-defense. Besides, he intended for yet another flagman to warn the engineer not to proceed, that there was danger ahead. If the engineer chose to ignore the warning, that was his option.

"How far we going, Jason?" Turner asked before he went back to work.

Jason squinted along the rails set on edge. That had been done by sheer muscle power. After the spikes were knocked loose, the rails were lifted off their ties and set on edge. He judged some nine hundred feet of rails were taken from their original settings. Another two or three rails would be enough.

"We'll get the next three, Sam," Jason replied. God, his hands were getting tender. It had been too long since he had engaged in hard physical labor.

Another rail was knocked loose from its bed of ties. They were brutally heavy, but there were many willing hands to lift them.

"That should do it," Jason said as the third

one was carried off. He straightened to ease his aching back. "Take all the bets you can get that the Rock Island won't pass through here tomorrow. Get your sledges back to Cummings."

"What are you going to do now?" Turner asked.

Jason smiled wearily at him. "Get to bed so I'll be able to move tomorrow. This is one circus I don't want to miss."

Turner cackled and whacked Jason on the ack. Jason managed to hide his wince. Sam was one tough old rooster.

Budd accompanied Jason to his rented room at Mrs. Lodges' boardinghouse. "Not luxurious, Arnold, but it'll have to do."

"It'll be just fine," Budd said as he began undressing. "Gonna be all hell to pay tomorrow."

"Yes," said Jason.

Budd had no trouble falling asleep, for Jason heard his soft snores shortly after he lay down. Jason wasn't as fortunate, however, for sleep kept evading him. He wished he could have seen April tonight, but the ride to Enid and back would have been too much. Then he thought of Budd saying that all hell was going to break loose. That was probably an understatement. In its outrage, the railroad would strike back like a wounded animal. The Rock Island's power was a different kind than the citizens of Pond Creek had ever been up against. This was legal power, silent but more punishing. Jason shook his head. There was only one thing in this whole mess that was in the people's favor. The railroad didn't know whom to single out to punish. It was up against a faceless mass. On that thought, Jason slipped away into slumber.

He and Budd had breakfast with Turner and several of the participants in the previous night's work. "Just forget about last night," Jason advised them. "After the wreck, and believe me there will be a big one, there'll be talk enough. We'll have aroused a sleeping beast, and the railroad will come up snarling and clawing. None of us will know what they're screaming about, so pass the word around. If the swipes of the Rock Island's mighty paws can't close on anybody in particular, that's all to our good."

Turner narrowed his eyes and studied Jason. "You're worried about this, aren't you, Jason?"

"Some," Jason admitted. "This isn't a matter of an engine making kindling out of an old house and some freight wagons. We're talking about a derailment with several kinds of damages following. We're talking about people being hurt and possibly killed. And we're talking about dragging the government right into this fight. Believe me, that will happen. The Rock Island will scream for the government to step in and settle this mess. The government will listen to that demand."

"It chews on you, doesn't it?"

"It chews," Jason said simply. "I've made a lot of good friends here, and I don't want to see anything happen to them."

"Maybe the railroad will give in and listen to our demands."

Jason bared his teeth. "About as quick as you gave in."

Turner ducked his head. "You made your point," he growled. "Now you've ruined my breakfast."

"Then we're in the same boat. Mine was ruined last night when I threw in with you."

Turner glanced at him from under lowered eyebrows. "You regret what you did?"

"I didn't say that," Jason corrected. "It was kind of exciting. I've got a hunch that what's about to happen is going to be a lot more exciting."

Half of the town was gathered near the track at train time. "Don't get any closer," Jason kept advising. "I don't know what will happen. I don't want any bystanders hurt."

He glanced at his watch. The scheduled north-bound freight train was about due. He was glad it was a freight. That meant no passengers, only crewmen.

He called the flagman over. "Get ready. Start running down the track when you hear the train. Be damned sure that engineer sees you waving the flag. We've got to be sure we're doing everything possible to warn him. If he's so hardheaded to keep on—" Jason's shrug broke off the words. "Then I'd say it's his own fault." His head lifted as he heard the distant wail of a train whistle. "Here it comes. Start running."

The flagman broke into a run, whipping the long staff of the makeshift flag back and forth.

Turner's eyes gleamed. "Only a blind man could miss that."

"It's the same flag used twice before," Jason warned.

Turner looked startled. "Are you suggesting that engineer might try busting on through?"

"I honestly don't know," Jason said.

Color spread through Turner's face, showing his anger was growing. "Then by God, I say let him smash himself all to hell if he's that stubborn."

All eyes were fixed on the approaching train. The engineer saw the flagman; Jason saw him wave cockily from the control cabin. There was no doubt that the engineer could see the on-edge rails. They had been moved off the ties. As Turner had pointed out, a blind man couldn't miss that. Everything depended upon the engineer's reaction to what he saw. He knew of the two prior attempts, as it had to be the talk among the train crews.

Jason was so tense he ached. Surely, the

engineer couldn't wrongly evaluate what he saw and think this was just another bluff. If he had orders that the train was to go through regardless of what he saw, then the railroad officials who had issued such orders were ignoramuses.

The engineer kept up a steady blast on his whistle, and it had an insulting sound to it.

The tenseness was getting to Turner, too, for he yelled, "You damned idiot! This ain't no joke. You'll see."

Jason's breath left him in an explosive whoosh as the engine ran off the firmly fixed rails and bumped across the ties, careening wildly. He was sure it would overturn, but it didn't. It ran over half of the section of wrecked rails before it ground to a halt. The freight cars piled up onto the engine like a heap of jackstraws. Several of them burst open; unfortunately, they were cattle cars. Cattle piled up everywhere. Several didn't get up and probably never would.

"You can celebrate now, Sam," Jason said in a shaky voice. "This is the first Rock Island train to stop in Pond Creek."

Turner gave him a sickly grin. Cattle poured out of the wrecked cars, and it was hard to hear over the animal bellowing. "It sure is," he said in a weak voice. "Kinda scares the hell out of a man, doesn't it?"

Jason nodded soberly. How right Turner was. But he could find relief in the aftermath. The train crew had gathered and, as far as Jason could see, there had been no injuries. The animal casualties, however, were another matter. As many as a hundred cattle probably wouldn't get up again. Somebody was going to be sued for this loss. The shipper would probably come down hard on the Rock Island.

The train crew was making futile efforts to round up the escaping animals, but there weren't enough of them. One of the harassed crewmen turned a red face toward Jason. "How about some of you giving us a hand in chasing down these cattle?"

"You cry real pitiful," Turner said sarcastically. "You didn't help us when our mail was scattered."

The crewman waited until he could speak, and his face kept growing redder. "All right, you bastards," he bellowed. "You'll pay for this. Wait and see."

"You accusing us of causing this?" Jason asked coldly. "Did you see us do it?"

Frustration turned the crewman's face ugly. "Maybe we didn't see you do it, but we're damned sure you did. We're not done yet. Just wait."

Jason turned away with Budd and Turner. "He keeps saying the same thing. Gets boring, doesn't it?" He grimaced at the obscenities flung after them. "Arnold, do you know what I'd like to do? I'd like to ride to Enid and see April. Do you realize how long it's been since I've seen her?"

"Long enough," Budd said in understanding.

"You're not going to be gone long, are you?" Turner asked.

Jason knew what Turner had in mind. He was afraid the railroad would start retaliation. "I'll be back before morning," he assured Turner, looking back as they walked away. The old man looked so forlorn.

"You frightened?" Budd asked.

"Not yet," Jason said calmly. "Just wondering what lies ahead."

It was almost suppertime when they dismounted before the Budd house. April met them at the door, and she flew into Jason's arms. "If you knew how I've worried," she cried.

"Couldn't help it, April. Had something that kept us tied up in Pond Creek until today. I'll tell you about it during supper."

April's face fell. "I didn't know you'd be here. I haven't got any food ready."

"You could fry some eggs," her father pointed out. "Wait until you hear about it. The biggest thing that's happened in this part of the country in a long while."

April fried eggs and ham and set out thick slices of homemade bread with preserves. "That'll have to do."

"It'll do just fine," Jason assured her. He ate rapidly for a few minutes. He hadn't realized until now just how hungry he was.

"What happened?" April demanded. "I've been pretty patient."

Jason laid down his fork. "We struck back at the Rock Island."

"Do you know what he did?" Budd broke in. "He derailed a whole train. By God, you wouldn't have believed it unless you saw it."

April's eyes grew rounder by the moment. "You didn't?" she gasped.

"Not by myself," Jason corrected. "A lot of other men helped. We pried up some rails. The engineer ignored our warning and tried to run through the section where they were gone. He found out in a hurry how wrong he was."

"Did the wreck hurt any people?" April asked in a subdued voice.

"It was a freight train. No passengers on it. Not even the crewmen were hurt." Jason shook his head. "A lot of cattle weren't as fortunate. I don't know how many were killed, but I'd say a hundred were injured."

April briefly closed her eyes. "How awful," she said in a barely audible voice.

Jason took that as censure, and his voice stiffened. "I regret it as much as you do, April, but there comes a time when a man has to do something drastic to make a point. We had to show the Rock Island we're dead serious about this."

April reached over and patted his hand. "I'm not blaming you. I know how you've been driven. Who will pay for the cattle?"

Jason shrugged. "I don't know. I imagine the shipper will sue the railroad. I can see no reason why the railroad won't have to pay."

"Will the railroad try to place the blame on you, Jason?"

He gave her a bleak grin. "They might try, but they have no proof."

"But if they try, could you go to jail?"

"Every man involved could go to jail. But as I said, there's no proof."

"But what if there is?" she persisted.

Jason picked up his fork, but his appetite seemed to have vanished. This conversation had turned grimmer than he wanted. April had a right to know all about everything that had happened, however, since both of her men were involved.

"I don't know what the railroad will do," he said patiently. "They may seek warrants to arrest the men who were responsible for the wreck, but there's no way they can name the perpetrators. No, the worst I can see happening is that the government will be called in." He couldn't keep the little note of triumph out of his voice. "Isn't that what we've wanted all along?"

CHAPTER NINE

The United States district attorney of Oklahoma Territory, Caleb R. Brooks, reread the telegram that had just been delivered. "I knew this was going to happen," he sighed.

His assistant, T. F. McMechans, looked up, startled. "What's eating on you, boss?"

Brooks had folded the telegram into a narrow piece of paper, and he tapped it against his thumbnail. "Just heard from Olney," he said tersely.

McMechans whistled. A telegram from the Attorney General in Washington meant trouble. "What's his problem?" he asked flippantly.

Brooks reproved him with a glance. Olney wasn't somebody to joke about. "The Rock Island Railroad registered complaints about the wreck in Pond Creek and demands that the government do something about it. Olney's ordering me to issue eighty warrants for the leading citizens there."

McMechans' jaw sagged. "How can he expect you to do that? You don't even know who took part."

"Olney is aware of that. But who am I to argue with the Attorney General? I'm to pick out the leading citizens. He says arresting them will

112

convince the rest of the futility of destructive tactics. Get the clerks busy making out those warrants."

"My God," the assistant wailed. "Who do I make them out for? I can't think of a single name of anybody living in Pond Creek."

"Get Marshal Nix in here," Brooks ordered. "He knows those people in Pond Creek."

Nix came into the office, his eyes wary. A command like this usually meant trouble. Although he was beginning to show his age, he still felt young enough to dress in flashy clothes, and his slicked-down hair was parted in the middle. He wore a jaunty mustache curled upward at the ends. "What kind of trouble is it this time?" he grunted.

Brooks grinned. "What makes you ask that?"

"Did I ever come in here to find anything else?" Nix countered.

"Did you hear about the train being derailed in Pond Creek?"

"How could I miss it? It's the talk of every saloon for miles around. I guess those Pond Creekers finally got tired of having their noses rubbed into the dirt. They hit back."

Brooks eyed him keenly. "Sounds like you sympathize with them."

"You got any objections to that?" Nix growled. "I know most of them. All solid, dependable people only fighting for their rights."

"You against the railroad?"

"They've been pretty high and mighty," said Nix. "Say, what's this all about?"

"I just received a telegram from Olney. He ordered me to issue warrants for eighty leading citizens of Pond Creek."

Nix's cheeks tightened, and he swore softly. "Now I get it. You want me to name names to put on those warrants."

"Are you refusing the Attorney General?" Brooks asked silkily.

Nix blinked. "Looks like I've got two choices. Either give you those names, or turn in my badge."

"You hit it right on the head; it's your decision."

Nix looked thoroughly unhappy. "You don't leave me any room, do you?"

"I'm just doing the job I was ordered to do," Brooks said mildly. "I expect you to do the same thing."

Nix muttered to himself. "Whom do I give these names to?"

"McMechans. He'll make out the warrants."

Nix made one last desperate effort to change the course of things. "Do you realize this is illegal? Swearing out warrants when there's no tangible evidence against those men?"

Brooks looked coldly at him. "Do you want to tell that to Olney?"

"Oh hell," Nix said in resignation. He crossed

to the table where McMechans sat. McMechans had a piece of paper before him and a couple of sharpened pencils. He looked sympathetically at Nix, but didn't comment.

Nix started naming people. He rolled off the most prominent people he knew first, but the page was only half-filled when his memor began to run dry. "How many do you have?" he asked.

McMechans counted the names. "Fifty-four."

Nix pulled at his fingers. "Won't that do?"

McMechans looked pained. "Olney said eighty. I guess he wants to teach these people a lesson."

"What about women?" Nix asked hopefully.

McMechans slammed his hand against the table. "You know damned well no women were involved in this. Do you want me to swear out a bunch of lies?"

"I don't see you doing anything else now," Nix said forlornly.

Brooks heard that remark. He crossed over to where the two men sat, and his face was frozen. "E.D., I think you might be getting too old for this job."

Nix swallowed hard. "I just thought of a few more names."

"I thought you would," Brooks said dryly. He went back to his work, and Nix called off some more names.

"One more," McMechans said after counting the list.

Nix was sure he knew more people in Pond Creek, but another name wouldn't come to mind. He thought harder, scowling fiercely. "Sam Turner," he said finally. It was a hell of a thing to do. Turner was an old man; he wouldn't be involved.

McMechans wrote down the name, dropped his pencil, and rubbed his cramped fingers. "I'll have the warrants ready this afternoon."

Nix nodded glumly. He wasn't pleased with himself for this bit of work. "How many deputies do you think I'll need?" he asked Brooks.

Brooks shrugged. "As many as you think necessary. I'd say eight or nine."

"No way. Pond Creek's got a taste of fight. I think they like it. Eight deputies won't come close to hemming them in."

Brooks looked curiously at him. "Do you think they'll fight the government?"

"I sure do. I think they'll start a civil war if they think the government is handing them a shabby deal."

Brooks flushed angrily. "I've got only one piece of advice for you, Marshal Nix. Why don't you stick to your job and let the government run the country?"

Nix stalked out of the office, his face set in grim lines. He went back to his own office and talked to his deputy, Pat Murphy.

Murphy listened judiciously to what Nix had to say, then offered, "I agree with what you say, E.D. Let's go and see what G. C. Daniels thinks."

Daniels was the Grant County attorney. His face grew longer as he listened to Nix's tirade. "I know how these people feel. What can they do, particularly with the government now against them? My advice is to go ahead and do what you're ordered to do."

Nix became livid. "Do you advise me to take a trainload of men to back up my authority? Do you realize what that's likely to do? That'd open up a bloody fight! No, I'd better appoint a few trusted men and go in to make an appeal to the citizens of Pond Creek." He pointed at Daniels. "I don't want any of this leaked out to the papers. I want this coming talk to be as peaceful as possible."

Daniels managed a strained grin. "Maybe we're lucky to have one sane man with us. Good luck, E.D."

Nix rode to Pond Creek with as little fanfare as possible. Four good deputies followed him. He had planned on having five, but Murphy had left a few hours earlier without telling him where he was going. Just before they reached Pond Creek, he saw him riding in the opposite direction.

Murphy raised a hand to stop Nix's outburst.

"Don't get sore, E.D. I rode over to get the lay of the land. Pond Creek is boiling. They're primed for battle. The story I get, the railroad somehow intercepted Olney's telegram, so they sent some of their men to tell Pond Creek that the government was coming to place the town under martial law."

"How'd they take that, Pat?"

Murphy grimaced. "Poorly. They're convinced that the government has turned against them and has sided with the railroad. I don't think you can talk any sense into them."

"I gotta try," Nix said. "I'm going on in alone. You wait here until you hear from me." He dismounted and plodded into town, his shoulders squared even though his head was bent.

Murphy sighed and shook his head. "He always had more guts than common sense. He's walking into a hornet's nest."

Nix walked down the main street. His step slowed as he saw a huge crowd of people just ahead. Everyone was armed with Winchesters and shotguns, waiting for what they thought would be an attack from a large bunch of deputy marshals. Nix's jaw firmed. It was going to take some straight talking to convince them otherwise.

He saw S. L. Bradley, the county clerk and recorder, and it startled him. He hadn't known

Bradley lived in Pond Creek. He carried a rifle, and he looked as determined as the others. "Lining up on the wrong side, aren't you, Bradley?" Nix asked mildly.

"This is my home," Bradley said flatly.

Nix's eyes roamed through the throng. Bradley obviously couldn't be reached. Maybe he could find a more reasonable man. "Jason," he said, picking out Keeler. "I thought you were too wise to get involved in this."

Jason raised an eyebrow at him. At least he wasn't hostile. "I thought so too, until the railroad called on the government for help. The government's backing the wrong side."

Nix nodded somberly. "My feelings exactly, Jason. Almost lost my job expressing them."

"We got rumors that the marshals are coming to arrest eighty of us."

"No rumor, Jason." Nix pulled the telegram from his pocket. "This came from the Attorney General. I think he's crazy, but who am I to tell him that?"

Jason admiringly shook his head. "I'll say one thing, E.D. Knowing all this then coming into town took a lot of nerve. Every gun here is aimed at you."

Nix's smile was strained. "That'd be a lot of wasted ammunition. It would only take one bullet." He thought that the belligerent undertone of the crowd had lessened.

Jason chuckled. "E.D., what are your thoughts on this?"

"I didn't come here to embarrass Pond Creek people. I've got all the respect in the world for them. Damn it, Jason, I'm trying to avoid using the martial force the Attorney General ordered." He shook his head. "The bigger a man gets, the more hollow his head seems to become."

A ripple of laughter ran through the crowd. Nix was slowly winning them over.

"You didn't come here just to tell us that," Jason said.

"No. I've got warrants for eighty of your people."

The laughter was suddenly all gone from the crowd. It was replaced by an ugly commotion.

Nix held up a hand. "I didn't say I came here to arrest anybody. I just said I had the warrants."

"You just try to use them," somebody in the crowd shouted.

Jason held up a hand. "What else is on your mind?"

"Like I said, I don't want to embarrass anybody. If your people step up as their names are called off, I'll check off the warrants and turn each man loose on his own recognizance if he agrees to appear before the United States commissioner at Kingfisher."

"Is there a hook hidden in this?" Jason asked, his eyes narrowed.

"Damn it, Jason," Nix said forlornly. "Where did you pick up all this suspicion? Can't you see you've got everything going for you? You can't be tried in Kingfisher. You've got a right to a trial in the county in which the act was committed. You'll be set free until you go up before a grand jury. I don't think a grand jury will act. Where's the witnesses against your men? This will give the railroad a tasteless cud to chew on."

Jason's lips twitched, then he broke into laughter. "Sounds like you've got it all figured out, E.D."

Nix sighed. He had averted a very dangerous potential riot. If that had broken out, nothing but the Army could have put the lid back on. "All right if I bring my deputies up, Jason?"

Several nos were screamed out of the crowd, but Jason paid no attention to them. "How many have you got, E.D.?"

"Six, counting myself," Nix answered gravely.

"Bring them up," Jason said. He turned furiously on the crowd. "Stop that damned yelling and cursing. Losing your heads now could stir up a bigger mess. You can thank Marshal Nix for keeping his head."

The commotion died to an unhappy murmur, then all was quiet.

Jason turned back to Nix. "I think you can go ahead with what you have to do, E.D."

"I'll never forget this," Nix said fervently.

Jason beamed. "You know something? Me neither. Your bosses might not realize it, but they sent the right man down here to stop any violence. This street could have been running blood."

Nix returned Jason's smile. "I've always been allergic to the sight of blood. Particularly when mine could have been involved."

Jason laughed and slapped his thigh. "Okay, men, let's get this over with."

Sam Turner was furious when he finally stepped forward. "This is just giving in to them," he mumbled. "I don't trust any of the breed that comes out of Washington."

Nix sighed as he checked off Turner's name. Hotheaded old cuss. His kind were always troublemakers. "Sam, you know me better than that. We've known each other a long time. Did I ever work against the people?"

"Not until now," Turner snarled.

Jason took hold of Turner's arm. "Shut up, Sam. Can't you see that Nix is doing us all a favor?"

"Favor, hell," Turner fumed as he turned away.

Nix finished his check-off and said, "Everybody can go home now. I'll have further information on what to do next."

Murphy stood beside Nix as they watched the crowd straggle away. "You don't know how close that was, E.D."

"Don't I?" Nix corrected. "I thought I'd have to change my undergarment."

"You going to tell Brooks how close this was?"

"You're damned right I am. If he wants to tell Olney about it, that suits me just fine."

"What do you think happens now?"

"I imagine Brooks will have to send in a bunch of deputies to round up the men on that list. I know one thing. He'd better handle it gently. There's no assurance this thing won't blow up again. Next time, we might not be so lucky."

CHAPTER TEN

The next day, Sam and Jason wandered down to the section of the track that had been destroyed. "By God, I can say one thing," Turner said proudly. "We bearded the lion in its own den."

"Yes, and that lion came out roaring," Jason remarked. "We're lucky so far, Sam. Our little action delayed two mail and passenger trains, but I don't think we're out of this mess yet."

Turner was staring down the track. An engine was backing a string of flatcars up to the break. "What the hell's that," he cried.

Jason noted that the flatcars were loaded with men and tools. "A work train. I imagine the Rock Island is preparing to restore its service. You didn't think it would be out long, did you?"

"I was just hoping it'd be forever," Turner said unhappily. He watched men clamber off the flatcars and drag tools with them. "How long do you think it will take them?"

"With all that manpower, I'd say it will be repaired before morning. Then the railroad can virtuously point out that they're doing their best to keep the tracks open."

"And the damned government will believe them," Turner said heatedly.

Jason looked sharply at him. "If you've got any

more crazy ideas in your head, you'd better get them out."

"It was your idea to take up the track," Turner said indignantly.

Jason squinted. "It was, wasn't it? I reached for something and got my hand slapped."

"So you're quitting," Turner said scornfully.

"I am for the time being. The railroad is a powerful corporation. Now they've got the government behind them." His attention was absorbed by the crew of the work train. "Watch and see how much power we're bucking."

Turner unwillingly watched the crew work. They already had the section of rails that were ripped out back in place and spiked down. "They still got to get that engine back on the track," Turner muttered.

"Didn't you notice that long-armed contrivance on the first car of the work train?" Jason asked. "It's a crane. It'll pick up the engine and have it back on the tracks almost as fast as they repaired the track. You're watching experts work, I'm afraid, Sam."

"It still won't change things," Turner said belligerently.

Once the track was repaired, the work train backed up until the crane was opposite the engine. The long arm swung out and men secured the huge chains.

"They'll never make it," Turner said.

"Don't bet on it," Jason advised.

There was tremendous power in that crane. The arm lifted, and the engine hung in the air. The crane moved a little and set the engine down on the track.

"I'll be damned," Turner muttered.

"Does *that* make you realize what you're up against?" Jason asked.

Turner's assurance had weakened. "There's still the freight cars to be set back on the track."

"They'll be handled easier than the engine," Jason observed. "They're not as heavy."

Car after car was lifted back onto the track and coupled to the engine. Some of them were so badly wrecked they had to be left temporarily where they were. It took even less time than Jason had thought. In only a few hours, the freight train was reassembled. An engineer climbed into the cab and got up steam. In a few moments it chugged off.

"Well, we caused them a lot of trouble," Turner said.

"Maybe not as much as we've caused ourselves," Jason remarked. "Oh, oh."

"What?" Turner asked, swiveling his head.

"Another train coming, Sam."

Hardly had the work train left when another train pulled into Pond Creek and stopped. It was the first time a train had done so voluntarily.

Jason had a sneaking suspicion as to why the

train arrived, and it didn't take long to solidify. Fifty marshals had come down from Kansas to round up the men whose names were on the warrants.

As hard as they looked, however, the marshals rounded up only sixty-five of the men. The rest had made themselves scarce. Sam Turner was conspicuously absent, Jason thought as he marched onto the train. He'd have believed Sam would go down fighting to the last.

Passing through a car, Jason saw Nix sitting in a seat near the front. He stopped beside him, and his expression was vindictive. "You didn't waste any time getting your marshals together."

Nix's face burned. "I knew you'd take it this way, Jason."

"What other way am I supposed to take it?" Jason snapped.

"It all happened before I was aware of what was going on," Nix said apologetically. "Brooks had it all set up when I got back to the office. He claims the railroad demanded fast action."

"Are you working for the railroad or the people?" Jason asked with a bite in his words.

Nix's jaws clamped together, then he said slowly, "Did you ever know me to cross the people?"

"Not until now," Jason said ungraciously, continuing on to the next car. He didn't want to sit near Nix. Instead, he found a seat across from Charles Curran, Pond Creek's city marshal. Jason shook his head. "Never thought they would take you, Charley."

Curran shrugged. "Why not? I helped remove those rails." He grinned bleakly. "Well, we can't say an injustice is being done. Almost every man in this bunch was in on that night. If I remember right, you were there, too."

"The whole thing was my idea," Jason said in a low voice. "I got tired of seeing Turner just fooling around."

Curran chuckled. "Sam's always got his hackles up. I'm glad he's not mad at me." He stared moodily out of the car window as the train began to move. "What happens now?"

Jason shrugged. "I guess we'll be jailed, though I don't think they've got a case. All this is a pure waste of time. They've got no witnesses."

"Do you think it's possible that the railroad will hire some liars to testify against us?"

"I wouldn't put anything beyond them," Jason replied.

"I hope they don't hold us long," Curran said. "With me gone, I don't know who's going to enforce law and order."

Jason chuckled. "We're a fair pair to be thinking of law and order. My work's going to pile up, too." Then there was the unhappy prospect of not seeing April for an indefinite time. He had to smile as he thought of how right April was to worry about him being jailed.

Finally, the train pulled into Kingfisher. The sheriff was there to meet it. Jason stepped down, and he saw the lawman's frown grow deeper as he studied the warrants Nix handed him.

"I can't arrest these men," the sheriff snapped. "These warrants aren't made out properly. Who exactly is bringing charges against them? Who are the witnesses?"

"Why, the Rock Island Railroad itself is the party bringing charges," Nix replied, his eyes gleaming. "Looks like somebody forgot something, Sheriff," he said softly. "What'll I do with these men?"

"You can't put them in my jail," the sheriff said firmly. "I suggest you put them in a hotel and hold them under guard while I do some telegraphing to straighten this out."

Nix walked over to talk to the Pond Creek men.

"How long do we have to stand out here?" Jason demanded.

Nix appeared to look pained. "There's been some kind of a mix-up. You'll be lodged in a hotel until it's straightened out." He thought a moment, then said softly, "You were wrong, Jason, when you thought I was crossing you."

"Looks like it, doesn't it?" Jason admitted, his eyes bright.

The marshals marched the group of men down the street to Kingfisher's biggest hotel and left them after making arrangements for their lodging.

It was a whole day before Nix returned. He found Jason, looked at his set face, and asked, "What's wrong now? You've got good accommodations and plenty to eat, and it's costing none of you a dime."

"It's going to cost somebody," Jason said flatly. "Who's paying for all this?"

Nix shrugged. "The government or the railroad."

"They'd better make up their minds soon," Jason said. "The men are getting restless. They want to get back home."

"They're going," Nix replied. "The telegraph wires have been hot between here and Herington, Kansas. That's where the railroad attorneys are, as I'm sure you remember when this all started. They've finally arranged to ship the prisoners back to Grant County, Oklahoma, to be tried before the grand jury under Circuit Judge Mackey. You know him?"

"I should," Jason answered. "I've tried some cases before him. Does the railroad know yet that they've lost their case? Without witnesses, Judge Mackey will throw them out of court."

"It's their fight," Nix said. "Anyway, the train will be leaving in less than an hour."

Judge Mackey was brief. "I see no reason to hold these men. The grand jury has looked into this matter and hasn't found solid legal grounds for these proceedings. Not a single witness has been presented. If the Rock Island insists on harassing these men, I warn them to have ample legal basis. Case dismissed."

Jason walked out with the free prisoners. He was lucky and knew it. He had engaged in an illegal pursuit of his own invention and gotten off scot-free. Next time, he might not be so fortunate. There easily could be witnesses that could help clamp a jail sentence around his neck. It was time to talk some sense into Sam Turner.

Nix walked into Brooks's office. Brooks looked up and said sourly, "Get that cat-licking-cream look off of your face."

"What does Olney say about what happened?"

Brooks looked through the papers on his desk. "I got a letter from him yesterday. Ah, here it is." He read from the letter:

"The citizens of Pond Creek took the law in their own hands. Fortunately, there was no human loss in the wreckage they caused, though I understand there was great destruction of railroad property, and two mail and passenger trains were delayed. Next week, I want there to be a hearing before the United States commissioner, charging some of the Pond Creek people with the obstructing and delaying of the mails. I'm sure a number will be bound over to the next term of court."

Brooks looked up sharply as Nix snorted. "I know how you feel," he said acidly. "I just finished writing Olney this letter." He cleared his throat before he read the pertinent part:

"All suspected parties have been released. The depredations were committed secretly. The people of Pond Creek will give no aid in naming the guilty parties, and the local authorities will not give assistance of any kind. They deplore what happened and assert their willingness to assist in suppressing the trouble, but are always ignorant of the identity of the guilty parties. Because the officers and citizens are all in sympathy with the guilty parties, it is impossible to secure proof or to get the law enforced. If the guilty parties could be arrested and have their cases heard outside these counties, I could soon break up this problem."

"What's the government going to do now?" Nix asked, a note of derision in his voice.

Brooks pursed his lips. "I don't know. If the railroad doesn't press it further, I imagine the matter will drop."

"The railroad better give up," Nix stated flatly. "And the trains had better start making two more stops. Some tough people live in those towns. They feel strongly their rights have been abused. I'll bet those so-called depredations will keep on."

"Then they're crazy," Brooks said. "Judge Mackey put them under bond not to touch railroad property again. The Rock Island has employed guards to patrol its track through and near Pond Creek. If they want a war, they can have one."

"You sound like you don't think they'll win."

It was Brooks's turn to look disdainful. "A mob against a powerful corporation? Don't be ridiculous."

Nix wanted to take him down a peg. "Who's going to pay for the lodging and feeding of the prisoners in Kingfisher?"

Brooks was momentarily taken aback. "The railroad or the government, I don't know."

Nix laughed sardonically. "Either way, that poor, helpless mob will have taken a good-sized bite out of a powerful corporation or the government." He pushed his hat to a more jaunty angle and strode out of the office. The last sound he heard was Brooks spluttering about his impudence.

CHAPTER ELEVEN

Jason unlocked his office door, opened it, and winced at what he saw. Just a week's absence from his normal routine seemed to tear everything to hell. His mail was piled up on the floor where the mailman had shoved it through the mail slot, and a thick patina of dust was over everything. Man didn't make a very lasting impression on any-thing, Jason thought as he removed his coat and prepared to sweep out the place.

He wielded the broom vigorously, coughing against the clouds of dust that rose from his efforts. He ought to get somebody in here on a regular basis, he mused as he finished sweeping the floor. The trouble was that he didn't know who. He discarded the kids he knew. Most of them were too irresponsible, their minds too filled with play rather than work. An older person wouldn't stoop to such menial work.

"I could do that," a voice from the doorway said.

Jason turned to see a slender man standing there. He judged him to be somewhere around twenty years old; his face was frank and open, and his grin was appealing. A lot of country showed in this man, yet Jason had the feeling this one was city-raised.

Jason smiled as he shook his head. "You must be hard up for a job to be asking for this one."

"I'm Clements Derry," the man said earnestly. "What I'm really looking for is a place to finish reading law in some office. I studied under Judge Garnet in Chicago."

Jason's face brightened. "The hell you did. I read law under him, too."

Derry nodded. "I know. He told me. When I heard about Oklahoma opening and decided to come here, the judge advised me to look you up." He grimaced at a memory. "He was a tough old coot. He could come down on you like he was squashing a bug. But he encouraged me to do my best. I never forgot what he said: 'Be honest and fair and never stop plowing ahead.' I should remember. I heard it often enough."

Jason laughed in delight. "He hammered that into a man's head hard enough, all right."

"Judge Garnet approved highly of you. He said I couldn't study under a better man."

Jason's delight increased. "It's good to get a compliment from that crusty old man, even though it comes secondhand. But I really haven't enough work to hire a man."

Jason had never seen anyone so eager. It fairly stuck out all over him. He started to shake his head, but Derry pleaded, "I could do all the housekeeping chores you're doing now. It'd leave you free for more important things."

No one could resist such earnestness. Jason laughed and gave in. "I couldn't pay much," he warned.

"Just enough for me to eat on."

Jason made the salary more than he intended. "You're hired, Clements. Five dollars a week."

"Give me that rag and let me show you a real duster."

Jason sat down and watched him. He wasn't very much older than Derry, but he couldn't begin to match him in energy. It might be just an early flare that would soon burn out, but Jason didn't care. He must be getting to be a man of influence. He had an employee. He didn't recognize the tune Derry was humming, but Jason felt like humming himself.

At the end of two weeks, Jason noticed a subtle change, growing more intense with each passing day. He didn't think Derry worked as vigorously, and it was a shock to realize that for the past three days he hadn't heard him humming. A flash in the pan, Jason thought unhappily. It wasn't that Derry was doing sloppy work, but his heart wasn't in what he did.

"Something bothering you, Clements?"

"Nothing," Derry mumbled.

"Must be," Jason insisted. "You're not the same man of two weeks ago."

Derry raised his head and met Jason's eyes

squarely. "There's nothing to do in this town, unless a man likes drinking. I'm not much of a drinker."

Jason studied him, then he had it. "Have you met any of our young ladies?" Jason asked softly.

The question put a sullenness in Derry's face. "I've met a couple. They were simpering, lifeless things."

Jason was more positive than ever that he knew what was bothering Derry. "You want more life in your women?"

Just the mention of it put a flame in Derry's eyes. "I don't think there's a woman like that anywhere in Pond Creek."

"Not that I know of," Jason agreed, then added, "But I know where some of those kind are."

Derry's nostrils pinched together with the rush of his breathing. "Where?"

"In Enid. In the Palace Saloon. Don't look so embarrassed. Or don't you think a saloon girl is good enough for you?"

Derry wouldn't look up. "I didn't mean it like that. It's just I've never been around a girl like that."

Jason thought of Ida Belle. "I don't think you'd find them simpering, lifeless things."

Derry still stared at the floor. "I don't think I want to make their acquaintance."

"Suit yourself," Jason said indifferently, and

went back to his work. He was only suggesting a relief for loneliness. Derry made it sound as though Jason was a partner in vice. The subject wasn't mentioned the rest of the day, but Derry was thinking about it. Jason could tell by the savagery with which he attacked his work.

Just before the office's closing, Derry approached him and asked, "Where is this Palace Saloon? I thought I might look it over."

"Fine," Jason said heartily, keeping all traces of humor off his face. A lot of the so-called good people around here, if they heard this conversation, would be horrified, seeing a fine young man led down the path to hell.

Jason didn't feel that way at all. He was only trying to help Derry cope with the natural impulses of life. He gave Derry instructions how to find the saloon and added, "Take Dandy. I won't be needing him tonight."

Derry shook his head. "I won't be going there tonight. Maybe someday out of curiosity, I'll look over the place." His face burned bright, and he breathed hard.

Oh, you liar, Jason thought in amusement. "If you do go, ask for Ida Belle," he added casually. "She's a cute little thing with a quick and facile mind."

He thought Derry was going to explode. "I told you I wasn't going there tonight." It was the sharpest tone Derry had ever used to Jason.

"Sure," Jason said laconically. Laughter was welling up inside him. He had to hold it or insult Derry. "You just mull over what I said, Clements. You'll change your mind."

"Good night," Derry said and walked toward the door.

I was wrong, Jason thought in amazement. All that talk hasn't touched him at all.

Derry paused at the door. "I've been doing some thinking. I don't think I want to study tonight. If your offer of using your horse is still good, I might take him."

"Fine, fine," Jason said, keeping a straight face. He'd bet there would be a change in Derry after tonight. For one thing, he would be more pleasant to be around.

Derry hemmed and hawed to clear his throat. "What was that girl's name?"

"Ida Belle," Jason answered soberly. "Be sure to mention you know me."

Derry wouldn't have to ask her name again. It was indelibly engraved on his mind. "Thanks, Jason."

"For what?" Jason asked in mock amazement. A broad smile broke out on Jason's face as the door closed. Meeting Ida Belle for the first time would be quite an experience. Jason almost envied him.

Derry pulled up before the saloon. His throat was tight, and he was having trouble with his breathing. His heart beat too fast, and it seemed as though there was a great hand around his chest, drawing tighter with every breath. He walked into the saloon, his expression diffident. He hadn't spent much time in saloons, and he wasn't quite sure how to act.

A big, redheaded woman came up to him and purred, "Looking for a good time, mister?"

This couldn't be the one Jason mentioned, and Derry shook his head. "I was looking for Ida Belle."

The woman's eyes clouded, and for some reason she almost appeared angry. "Most of the new ones do," she said harshly. "Ida Belle," she called. "Somebody here asking for you."

A slender, small blonde turned away from the bar and approached Derry. Her pert face was expectant. "Yes?" she asked.

How difficult it was to talk. "I'm Clements Derry," he mumbled. "Jason told me to mention his name."

Her eyes were magnificent. "You know Jason?" she asked eagerly.

Evidently, the name meant something to her. "I work for him," Derry replied.

"Isn't that fine!" she exclaimed. "Quite a while back, Jason used to wander in here. I haven't seen him for a long time." Could that be a wistful quality in her voice? She seemed to shake off some memory, for she said, "Come over here and let's sit down. I want you to tell me about him."

She was amazingly shapely for a woman with so small a figure. Her dress was cut low, and Derry kept swallowing hard as he looked at the low-cut bodice. He wouldn't call her beautiful, but there was an endearing quality in that impish face.

Ida Belle led him over to a table and sat down. Derry appeared hesitant, and she laughed, "Sit down. I won't bite." She waited until Derry awkwardly seated himself. "What was your name?"

"Clements Derry," he replied. How his pulses beat. He hadn't met a woman like her in all his life. Her eyes sparkled, and she laughed frequently.

"It's a nice name," she murmured.

"So's Ida Belle," he blurted out.

She shrugged her expressive shoulders. "I didn't have much choice picking it out. I guess I've grown used to it. Do you want a drink?"

"Whatever you recommend," he said huskily.

"I usually drink bourbon."

"That'll be fine for me, too."

"I'll be right back," she said and rose.

He didn't take his eyes off her until she returned to the table. Before she could sit down, a big, burly man approached her and said, "I've been waiting for you, Ida Belle."

"Not now, Mike," she said sharply.

Derry felt an unexplained stab of jealousy until the big man left. "He sounded disappointed," he remarked.

Again those smooth shoulders shrugged. "He'll get over it," she said lightly.

She raised her glass. "To a newfound friend." She almost drained it in one gulp.

Derry tried to imitate her. The liquor seemed harsh, with a bite. He was choking when he set the glass down.

Her eyes sharpened. "You don't have to take it so fast."

He stubbornly shook his head. He could keep up with anything she did. But he noticed she didn't finish her drink. He didn't know much about saloon girls, but he thought they made their money out of a percentage of the drinks they sold to the customer. If that assumption was correct, then Ida Belle was making little money on him. Things began to swim before his eyes, and her face grew blurry. "I want you to be honest with me," he said thickly.

"You know I will," she said softly.

"You'd be making more money if that Mike was with you."

Her eyes crinkled in amusement. This Derry didn't miss much. "I might've," she admitted. "But that's two different things."

Derry stubbornly shook his head. He wasn't going to appear less in this girl's eyes. "No," he said, his voice rising, "I can drink as much as any other man."

She reached out and patted his hand. "Sure you can," she soothed. "But in this case, you don't have to."

"I want another drink, Ida Belle," he said, his voice growing sharper. "If I can't have it, it's proof you don't want me around."

Ida Belle sighed. Derry's words were becoming slurred. He was a novice at drinking, and she knew from experience how much trouble that kind could cause. He stared at her with so much pleading in his eyes that she gave in. "All right, Clements," she said, and walked to the bar.

Trevlin frowned at her. "Your new boyfriend is getting kinda loud, isn't he?"

"I guess the drink was too strong," she said ruefully.

Trevlin's eyebrows rose. "He gets that way on one drink? You keep a close eye on him. If he gets louder or starts to make trouble, I'll pitch him out so fast it'll make his head swim."

"I'll watch him, Slim," Ida Belle promised. "Two more drinks. Make them light."

Trevlin laughed sardonically as he poured the two drinks.

Ida Belle came back to the table. "Now, take this one slow," she said gently.

She tried to pace him by setting an example. She felt a growing liking for him. Maybe it had started because he said he worked for Jason. Now it was a different thing. He had a gay and infectious laugh and he had made her laugh until tears streamed from her eyes. He had a humorous way of putting things, and he recounted stories of his childhood that aroused peal after peal of laughter from her. Ida Belle could tell a good story, too, and she told him how she'd grown up, skipping the distressing parts.

Derry chuckled as she finished another incident. "You know, I never had so much fun in my life."

To her amazement, Ida Belle could say the same thing. She could honestly say she liked him.

"You know something, Ida Belle? My glass is empty."

"You don't need another drink," she said.

That stubbornness was touching his face again. "And have you think I'm a tightwad? You couldn't have made any money off me so far. I want another drink."

She knew that arguing with him would be unwise, for he could get loud. That would arouse Trevlin to action. Ida Belle didn't want that.

"Well, maybe another one," she granted. She would see that the drink was weak.

She smiled to herself as she came back with the drinks. Derry was the only one worrying about her not making any money. She was enjoying herself. It had been a long time since she had met someone she thoroughly enjoyed. Not since Jason, she thought in nostalgia.

Despite her efforts, Derry kept insisting he order more drinks. He got five of them down; despite their being weak, they were having their effect. As he kept getting louder, it aroused amusement all over the room. But Trevlin wasn't grinning. His frown grew more set.

"Clements," she said suddenly, "I've got a splitting headache. I think I'd better go home."

"I talked too much," Derry said in instant distress.

"Not that at all," she said gently. He was the serious kind, taking blame when there was none. She had to do something to erase all sense of guilt from his mind. "Will you walk me home?"

His face brightened. "It'd be my pleasure," he said thickly.

She didn't let him know she was supporting him, but his steps were unsteady. A block from her room he groaned and said, "I'm going to be sick."

He moved out to the middle of the street, and his stomach emptied. He came back to where she waited, and his face was a peculiar green. "I'm so sorry," he said miserably.

"Why?" she asked practically. "I've seen men sick from liquor before."

He kept apologizing all the way to her stairs. He kept clutching at the banister every other step.

"You all right, Clements?" she asked anxiously.

His head hung low, and he mumbled so badly she barely made out his words. "I don't feel so good, Ida Belle."

She thought he would fall before she got him inside. With her support, he managed to make it to the old worn sofa. He was too long to fit comfortably, but it didn't matter. He was asleep the moment his head touched it.

She tugged off his boots and looked down at him, her lips curving in a soft smile. Poor baby, she thought. He was trying to prove he could drink with the regulars who came into the Palace. She stared at the helpless, sleeping face and a strange tenderness filled her. She shook herself brusquely as she removed a blanket from her bed, unfolded it, and spread it out over him.

Derry fought his coming back to wakefulness. He kept his eyes tightly closed, for he knew if he opened them the top of his head would come off. Finally, he opened them a small crack at a time, then howled and grabbed his head.

"Feel bad?" a sympathetic voice asked.

He opened his eyes cautiously again. Ida Belle was standing beside him. "Where am I?" he asked wildly.

"In my room," she answered matter-of-factly. "Don't you remember offering to take me home?"

Maybe he vaguely remembered that. "A little," he said.

"You were sick on the way here. I barely managed to get you on the couch before you passed out."

Derry looked at the blanket covering him. "You covered me up?"

"I thought I'd better," she said calmly. A smile moved across her face. "You learned something last night."

"What was that?"

"That you can't drink."

He groaned at the unpleasant memory.

"I was trying to keep from completely ruining your evening. You were kind enough to sit and talk to me."

"It was my pleasure," she assured him.

He remembered something else, for he yelped. "Now what?"

"I rode Jason's horse over here. I left him tied outside the saloon. Oh my God, he'll never forgive me."

Ida Belle shook her head. "That's one worry you can throw away. I saw Dandy as we passed. I know Jason's horse. After you fell asleep, I came back out and led him to the livery stable."

He stared at her in complete disbelief. "Do you know you're a wonder?"

She tried to shrug off the praise but a telltale

blush stained her cheeks. "What good is a friend if she can't help another friend?"

He flushed. He hadn't thoroughly disgraced himself, or she wouldn't be talking this way. Then his eyes widened as they took in the strange room. "I spent the night here, in your room?"

"It seemed the only logical thing to do."

"But I shouldn't have done that," he protested wildly. "What will people think if they hear about it?"

She didn't tell him that a saloon girl didn't have much of a reputation to be concerned about. "Don't worry about it," she said cheerfully. "Maybe it'll never get out. How do you feel?"

He sat up. "Awful. My stomach's queasy, my head aches."

"The usual aftermath of a person's first bout with whiskey," she observed. "I'll fix some breakfast."

Derry shuddered at the word. "I couldn't eat a mouthful."

"Maybe you know best," she said uncertainly. "But a cup of coffee will help."

She was trying so hard to be helpful that Derry gave in. "Well, maybe," he said doubtfully. "What time is it?" He moaned when she told him. "I've got to get back to Pond Creek! Jason will be worried if I'm gone much longer."

"Jason knew where you were, didn't he?" At his nod, she continued, "Then he won't be worried."

She prepared the cup of coffee, and Derry's stomach almost rebelled just at the aroma. "Get it down," she advised him. "It'll help. You'll see."

He took it in cautious sips while she watched anxiously. He finished the cup, and it seemed to settle his stomach. "Better," he said, trying to smile. "I'll never do that again."

"That's wise," she approved. Then some further thought put distress on his face and she asked, "Now what?"

"I won't be able to see you again. I won't be able to come into the saloon."

"Why not?" she demanded. "We can just talk. You can drink sarsaparilla, can't you?"

He stared at her in awe. "You mean you'd want to see me again after this fiasco?"

"I suggested it, didn't I?"

Derry tugged on his boots, and Ida Belle walked to the door with him. "Take it easy," she advised, then planted a quick kiss on his cheek.

"Do you know you're something?"

"Tell me about it the next time you come in," she said and smiled.

It was almost eleven o'clock in the morning when Derry entered Jason's office. His step dragged, and he stared at the floor.

Jason didn't notice those things at first. He was annoyed at Derry's tardiness. "I thought you'd forgotten where you worked," he said with an edge to his voice.

"I'm sorry I'm late, Jason," Derry mumbled. He made another attempt to speak, broke off, sighed, then said, "You might as well know the whole story."

"I'd appreciate that," Jason said sarcastically.

"I spent the night with Ida Belle," Derry said faintly.

Jason frowned, then he laughed. "You mean in the saloon? I didn't think she worked all night."

Derry wouldn't look at him. "She didn't. I took her home." He darted a furtive glance at Jason. "I spent the rest of the night there."

Jason whistled in surprise. "You're better than I gave you credit for."

Derry's face flamed. "It's not what you're thinking. I guess I drank too much whiskey. I was sick on the way to her room. I barely got inside when everything went black."

Jason was grinning broadly. "You really hit it hard, eh?"

"I was mortified when I woke up this morning. I thought Ida Belle would be furious with me. She wasn't. I can come back and see her again."

"But you're not going to," Jason guessed. "You don't want any more drinking bouts?"

"I'm going back," Derry said stubbornly. "Ida Belle said we could sit and talk. I can drink sarsaparilla."

"And you're going?"

"I am," Derry said firmly. "I never met a girl like her." He could look at Jason now. "She told me of you rescuing her from that railroad man."

"She didn't take much rescuing," Jason said, and chuckled. "She and her friends had things pretty well under control."

Derry's face darkened. "I wish I'd been there. I'd have knocked his head off."

"Then last night might not have happened," Jason said practically.

Derry looked startled. "Say! That's right. Ida Belle says that's when all the trouble with the railroad started."

"Just about that time," Jason said thoughtfully. "But it was bound to happen sooner or later."

"Are you saying that the railroad is to blame, Jason?"

"You're damned right I am. That railroad doesn't want to give the service they should to Enid and Pond Creek. They're trying to force the towns to move back to where the railroad originally built their depots. The people have refused, and there's been bad feelings ever since."

"Were you in on the wrecking of that train?"

"In on it?" Jason laughed shortly. "I was the one who thought of it. That's just between you and me," he said hastily.

"Not a word," Derry promised. "Was the aftermath serious?"

"I thought I was going to jail for my part, Clements. I was even arrested and taken to Kingfisher. The sheriff there refused to jail us. We were sent back to Oklahoma and tried before a grand jury under Judge Mackey. He freed us." Jason shook his head. "I learned a lesson. The railroad is big and tough. Maybe too tough for a few townspeople to buck. From now on, I'm keeping my nose out of it. But it's not over, not by a long shot. The Rock Island is patrolling the right-of-way with paid guards. The court issued an injunction to the people of Pond Creek not to touch railroad property. So far, it's been quiet, but that's only a surface calm. I look for the lid to blow off at any time. Do you know Sam Turner?"

Derry shook his head.

"Sam's the kind that won't let it lay. He feels he's been personally abused, and he's taken on a personal vendetta against the railroad." Jason shook his head. "The only way to lay that vendetta is to kill him or jail him. I wouldn't want to see either one happen. Despite his irascible temper, Sam's a likable old cuss."

"Ida Belle start all this?" Derry asked in awe.

Jason nodded solemnly. "In a way she did. That railroad man, Kevan, vowed Enid and Pond Creek would be damned sorry." His eyes narrowed, and he muttered, "I wonder how much of this trouble is due to Kevan?" Then he shook his head. "Naw, he's not that big."

"Will it end?" Derry asked.

"It has to end one way or the other."

"The railroad will come out on top?"

"I'm afraid so," Jason said unhappily. "It's a big and powerful corporation. The government could break it up, but so far it's been on the railroad's side."

He turned back to his work and picked up a letter. Derry started the dusting, snapping the dustcloth after each swipe. He filled the air with dust, and Jason choked on it.

"Hold it!" he yelled. "If one night with Ida Belle does this for you, I'd hate to see what several in a row would do."

Derry grinned abashedly, but his eyes were glowing. "You know, I can't get her out of my mind."

"It shows," Jason said dryly.

Derry started dusting again, but his attention wasn't on it. The dustcloth moved slowly, and his eyes were far away.

Jason laid his letter aside. He wasn't going to get any work done until this was settled. "Now, what's eating you?"

"Jason, I was just wondering if I could borrow Dandy again?"

"You can't spend every night in the Palace," Jason said sternly. "You're not earning that kind of money."

"I've got a little money saved up," Derry said stubbornly. "I just have to see her again."

Jason whistled soundlessly. It couldn't happen in just one evening, but Derry seemed smitten. He might as well let him have Dandy. Derry wasn't going to settle down until he got this out of his system, or at least under a semblance of control.

"Don't you stay out all night again," Jason ordered.

"I won't." Derry's eyes were shining. "Thanks, Jason."

"Forget it." Jason picked up the letter again. He had to make some intelligent reply, and he couldn't if he kept thinking about Derry. He laid the letter down again. Ah, that first surge of attraction. It was too bad that it couldn't last longer. Did he regret that he had steered Derry onto Ida Belle? No, he decided. Every young man should know somebody like Ida Belle. Derry would get it out of his system.

CHAPTER TWELVE

Sam Turner lay in the tall grass along the right-of-way. It was dark, and his eyes glittered as he watched the railroad guard march along the track. "You bastard," he muttered angrily. He still quivered with indignation every time he thought of the Rock Island not stopping at Pond Creek. "I'll show them," he said.

Lucas Morrow squirmed uneasily beside Turner. He had never seen anybody so eaten up. Turner hadn't better press his obsession any further. The courts were on the railroad's side now. "Sam," he said in a shaky voice, "you know what the court said about damaging any more railroad property."

"I ain't going to damage any of their property," Turner snarled. "But by God, the trains are going to stop here. I'll see to that." He was working himself into a rage, and it showed in his face and voice.

The guard had reached the limit of his patrol and was turning back. He carried a lantern.

"Look at him strut," Turner growled. He had brought a Winchester with him, and he lifted it from the ground and snugged the butt against his shoulder.

"What are you doing?" Morrow whispered, his voice hoarse with alarm. "Sam, you can't—"

"The hell I can't. I'm still sick and tired of being kicked around. If I've got to start showing the railroad how I feel, I'll start with the small ones first." He squeezed the trigger.

The sharp crack of the rifle resounded in the still air. The lantern globe exploded into small bits. The guard dropped the shattered lantern, and his hoarse squawk of terror sounded loud. He didn't look around to locate his attacker, but fled into the darkness.

Turner cackled with obscene delight. "Hell, he won't stop until he hits Kansas."

Morrow's expression was worried. "Tell me what good you did, Sam."

"Scared the hell out of that one, didn't I? When that guard reports to the others, it'll scare them, too. Now, I'll think of something else to annoy the railroad."

"You're going to think yourself into jail," Morrow said.

"You let me worry about that," Turner replied. He hoisted himself up off the ground, cradling his rifle. "I'm thirsty. How about a drink? Brown's is the closest."

"Maybe it'll help simmer you down," Morrow said in relief. He and Turner had been friends for years, but the last one seemed to have brought out all the worst in the old man.

Only a half-dozen men were in Brown's. They looked up at Turner and Morrow's entrance and one of them said, "What's the rifle for, Sam? You sure ain't hunting tonight."

Again, that obscene cackle sound. "I was doing a little hunting tonight, as a matter of fact. Just missed getting me a railroad gunkus. It's a two-legged animal with a wide streak of yellow down its back."

"You funning us, Sam?" the same man asked. "I never heard of any such animal."

"It wasn't funny, Jim," Morrow said sourly. "He took a shot at one of the railroad guards."

Eyes grew round as men stared at Turner. "No!" several of them exclaimed.

"I didn't take a shot at a guard," Turner said indignantly. "I ain't that poor a shot. I shot at his lantern. Busted it all to hell." His laugh rang out again. "He must have some greyhound in him, the way he took off."

All along the bar heads were shaking in disapproval. Brown leaned across the bar, angry. "Sam, you keep on and sure as hell you're gonna get yourself locked up. You know what that judge said about destroying railroad property?"

The criticism stung Turner. He had failed twice before these judging eyes, once with the house and again with the wagons. "I didn't destroy any property," he howled.

"He busted that lantern, didn't he, Morrow?"

Morrow bobbed his head. "Blew it all to hell."

"That was railroad property," Brown insisted.

"Do you know what could happen to you if some smart railroad lawyer got ahold of that?"

Turner's eyes were burning. He had made a public vow that he would see Rock Island trains stop at Pond Creek. So far, he hadn't come close.

"I'll show you," he yelled in a choked voice. "You wait and see." He turned and plunged out of the saloon.

"I've known Sam too long," Morrow said. "He's got an obsession. Somebody's gonna get hurt before this is settled."

"You better stay away from him," Brown observed. "He's liable to pull you in over your head."

"Not me," Morrow said sorrowfully. "He picked out this horse to ride. If it throws him and breaks his neck, that's his lookout." He shook his head. "I'd sure hate to see that happen."

"Then you'd better do something about it," Brown said brusquely. "Do you know Jason Keeler?"

"The lawyer? Sure, I know him."

"Does he have any influence left with Turner?"

"I don't know." Morrow's face was all screwed up.

"You'd better talk to him before Turner gets into trouble so deep he can't get out."

Morrow pushed away from the bar. "Maybe

Keeler is still at his office. I don't know where he lives."

Every head gave him a negative shake. They didn't know where Keeler lived, either.

"I'll go by his office," Morrow said.

He hurried down the street, and an explosive "Good" burst from his lips as he saw the light in the window. Somebody was working late. He rapped on the door, and Jason answered.

"Jason, I'm sorry to bother you, but I'm worried. I won't be but a few minutes."

"Come in." Jason stepped out of the way. "What can I do for you?"

Morrow sat down. "It's about Sam, Sam Turner."

"What's he done now?" Jason said crisply.

Morrow briefly related the shooting of the guard's lantern and Turner's vow that he wasn't stopping there. "He's got all his friends worried. He's got this crazy grudge against the railroad, and we're afraid he'll get in over his head."

"That could easily happen," Jason said grimly. "The railroad would dearly love to get their hands on a perpetrator of some of the crimes against them. They'd hang him up to dry. That damned Sam. Once he gets an idea lodged in his mind, nothing can knock it out."

"Will you talk to him?" Morrow begged.

"I'll try." Jason's shaking head said he doubted any definite results would come out of the conversation. "I've been critical of Sam. We're not as close as we once were."

"But you'll try to dissuade him from the road he insists on taking?"

"I promise I'll do my best."

Jason's face was troubled as he watched Morrow leave the office. He wished he felt as certain as Morrow looked.

The next morning, Jason found Turner working on a small structure just off the tracks. "Sam," he greeted him, "you sure put that up in a hurry. What is it?"

"It's a depot," Turner answered in a surly tone. "I spent most of the night cutting the boards to fit. I hauled it down here shortly after dawn."

Jason gave him a puzzled frown. "A depot? What for?"

Turner threw down his hammer. "It'll stop those damned trains," he shouted, "that's what it will do. When I'm finished, I've got a sign to paint on it. I'm sick and tired of everybody laughing at me because I vowed the Rock Island will stop here. I keep my promises."

Jason shook his head. "It won't work, Sam," he said gently. "Even if the engineer sees your depot, he'll roar on by without even slowing down."

That dire prediction didn't ruffle Turner. "He'll stop all right," he said complacently.

"What makes you so positive, Sam?"

"I put some dynamite caps on the track. The reports of them going off will slow down that engineer. Seeing the depot will stop him." He picked up his hammer. "Just get out of my way, Jason. I've got some work to finish."

Jason stepped back reluctantly. If the railroad could single out Turner as the chief perpetrator of the harassing tactics, some jail cell would hold him for a long time.

Sam nailed the last board into place, then picked up a paint pot and brush. He painted "Depot" on the front of the shack over the large opening that ran across the building. Then, in smaller letters, he painted "All trains stop here." He stepped back to survey his work, humming to himself.

Jason felt so damned sorry for the old man.

"What do you think of that, Jason?" Turner crowed.

"I think it won't work," Jason said flatly.

Red crept up Turner's neck. "You're such a know-it-all," he howled. "The train's due here in less than an hour. Stick around and see what happens."

"I will, Sam."

So would quite a number of other people. News of Turner's latest project had spread fast, for they were already trickling to the scene. Turner's scheme had no chance of working; the crudely painted sign wouldn't fool the rawest of novice engineers. Poor Sam, Jason thought. He had opened the doors even wider to admit a greater flood of ridicule.

From somewhere Sam had secured an agent's cap. He sat on a box behind the large opening in the shack. He might think he looked like an official agent, but he didn't. Any real employee of the railroad wouldn't be fooled for a moment by this trickery.

Half of Pond Creek had gathered by the time the train was heard in the distance. Several hundred yards from the make-believe depot, Jason heard the first of the dynamite caps go off, followed by a half dozen more. It might have startled the engineer, but he didn't slow down. He roared on by the false depot, leaning far out to wave at its self-appointed agent. Turner came out of the depot, his face twisted with wrath, screaming after the disappearing train.

The laughter came then, a snicker and a chuckle at first, then welling into roar after roar. Men slapped their companions on the back and pointed derisive fingers at Turner. Jason felt sick at heart for the old man. This was public humiliation of the worst kind. That derisive laughter was enough to shrivel a man's soul.

"Laugh, damn you!" Turner raged. "If some of you had pitched in, it would've worked."

"Turner," somebody in the crowd yelled, "why don't you give it up? You're only making a fool of yourself. Every time you try one of your fool schemes, the railroad comes out looking stronger than ever."

Turner visibly weakened. His shoulders slumped, and his hands hung helplessly at his sides. A crowd could be the cruelest thing in the world. Most of them had suffered a great deal under the railroad's handling, and now they took their frustration out on an old man.

Jason approached him. "Come on, Sam," he said gently. "I'll help you put away your tools. What are you going to do with the depot?"

"Let it stand there," Turner said grimly. "It'll be a public monument to this town's cowardice. Every time they see it, it'll be another slap in the face."

"Sure, Sam. We'll do just that," Jason answered, not even intending to consider Turner's proposal. Sometime during the night he would gather a few of the more sane men and tear the structure down.

But he couldn't do anything about the laughter. Every time Turner appeared, it would only break out anew. A pack of hounds had spotted its prey. It would never cease its baying until the prey had been run down and destroyed.

CHAPTER THIRTEEN

Derry had such an air of expectancy on his face that Jason knew what he wanted before he opened his mouth. "No, Clements," he said firmly. "I plan to use Dandy myself tonight." He had never seen a man look so sick. "I've got to see April. Rent a horse from the livery stable."

Derry brightened. "I guess I could do that," he said. But something still bothered him.

Jason wondered if it could be a lack of money. Derry was spending a lot of evenings at the saloon, and that wasn't cheap. He considered speaking to him about this, then decided against it. Derry wasn't of legal age, but he was old enough to make his own decisions. It was still just a bad case of puppy love. Then he remembered all of Ida Belle's endearing qualities, and it was entirely possible that Derry might be smitten enough to overlook her background.

Jason thought about it all the way to Enid. Was Derry crazy enough to ask Ida Belle to marry him? More importantly, would she agree? Now there was a crazy thought! The entire matter was too ridiculous even to think about.

Budd answered his knock on the door. "I want to talk to you, Jason. All hell is popping around here."

Jason saw April smiling at him over Budd's shoulder. "Later, Arnold. I've got something a lot more important on my mind right now." He brushed by Budd and approached April, his arms extended wide. She came into them, her face lifted to him.

"It seems so long since I've seen you, Jason," she whispered.

He bent his head to kiss her. "It seems longer to me, April." He stepped back, still holding her hand. "Anyway, I've got to talk to you." He looked back at Budd, standing near the door. "Arnold, I'm not cutting you out. I might need your advice."

They sat down, and Jason addressed them both: "Neither of you knows Clements Derry. He's the man I've taken on to read law."

April and Arnold shook their heads.

"Something's come up that's beginning to make me worry," Jason went on. "Clements is spending a great deal of time at the Palace Saloon. He's seeing Ida Belle as often as he can." He half-expected a wave of resentment to wash across April's face, and to his surprise it didn't come.

"I think I know him by sight," April said. "Three times, I saw a tall, thin man walking about town with Ida Belle. His feeling for her shows plainly. Twice he was holding her hand."

"That's what has me worried," Jason said. "I'm afraid he's getting too involved with her."

"You mean enough to marry a saloon girl?" Budd asked unbelievingly.

"It could happen if he goes on like this. How would you handle it? Kick him out and tell him he's on his own?"

April frowned at him. "I never expected such narrow-mindedness from you, Jason. We had a situation like this once in our family, didn't we, Papa?"

Budd looked startled. "Lord, that was so long ago, I'd almost forgotten about it. I didn't think you knew. You were just a kid."

April smiled impishly at him. "You'd be surprised at how much kids learn. We used to snicker a lot over Uncle Henry and his romance. He cared enough for Aunt Martha to go ahead and marry a girl who worked in a saloon."

Budd turned brick-red. "Here now," he protested, "we didn't talk about things like that in our family."

April giggled. "Oh, the family talked about it some, particularly when the menfolk weren't around." She winked at Jason. "Maybe knowing about Uncle Henry was what worried me about you and Ida Belle. Do you know something? Martha made Uncle Henry a devoted wife. He never had to worry about her turning her head to glance at a passing man. Maybe working in a saloon she had gotten her fill of men. The kids were crazy about her. Even the women had almost forgiven her before she died. I don't think Uncle Henry ever regretted a single moment of being married to Martha. Occasionally some loudmouth would make an unwise remark about Martha and Uncle Henry would come home marked up, but by the pleased shine in his eyes I don't think he ever lost a fight. I'd hear Martha scold him as she patched him up, but the pride shone out of her eyes." She looked at her father. "Didn't you like her, Papa?"

"Nobody could help liking Martha," Budd said gruffly. "All this time I didn't know you knew about her background."

"Her background didn't matter," April said softly. "It was the goodness within her. A lot of people grieved for her when she passed away a couple of years ago. I'd be happy to have so many sincere mourners."

"You will," Jason asserted. "But that's a long time away. Anyway, I won't try to steer Derry off if it's Ida Belle he wants. He might turn out as lucky as Uncle Henry." He smiled at Budd. "What's bearing on your mind so heavily, Arnold?"

Budd had a heavy, unhappy look. "The same old trouble. That damned railroad is getting mightier and mightier. The townspeople are getting fidgety again. I've heard they discussed tearing up the track in Enid. Fortunately, a few of the calmer heads talked them out of that craziness, pointing out how it had turned out in Pond Creek."

"I'm glad they did," Jason said earnestly.

"But those calmer heads weren't enough to completely stop them," Budd muttered, "even though Deputy Sheriff Miller promised the crowd he'd arrest anybody who dared touch the track."

"Didn't that check them?" Jason asked in amazement.

"I've never seen such zealots," Budd complained. "While Miller was talking to the crowd, a few slipped away and soaked the railroad bridge with coal oil. Then they doused a bale of hay with the stuff and set it against the timbers and fired the bale. Luckily, Miller saw the glow in the distance and got to the spot in time to kick the burning bale aside. He got the rest of the fire out before it had seriously burned the bridge support. I never saw a man so furious. He raved and cussed, promising dire results to every man within reach of his voice. They just jeered at him. I'm telling you, Jason, if this fight isn't ended soon, all law and order is going to disappear. Its going to be pure anarchy."

Budd pulled at his knuckles. "Even with all this trouble, trains keep whistling through town. The people have used red lanterns and dynamite caps on the tracks. A few of the more daring have actually fired bullets at the passing trains. Somebody's going to get killed. A couple of days ago, I sat at a meeting that passed an ordinance making it a violation for a train to pass through Enid without stopping. We couldn't enforce it." He threw up his hands. "How can you arrest an engineer within the city limits while he's on a train traveling fifty miles an hour?"

Jason's eyes sharpened. "I heard a story about a runaway caboose the other day. What happened with that?"

Arnold sat forward. "Three city policemen saw a caboose that had broken loose from a southbound freight. They rushed it, and tried to place the crew under arrest. The conductor, brakeman, and several other railroad employees fought back with gun butts and clubs. Then the engineer backed up the train to the caboose and coupled with it. He opened the throttle, and the train roared away. The policemen had no chance to get off. The train didn't stop until it reached Hennessey, where the luckless officers, bruised and beaten, were thrown off. Enid went crazy. A charge of resisting Enid's law was placed against the Rock Island. We had another meeting, and the council swore to halt the Rock Island if it had to deputize every man in the city."

Jason's fingers drummed on the arm of his chair. "We've got to ask the government to intercede again. I know they haven't been favorable to our side yet, but after so much trouble they've got to change their views. We'll start up a petition demanding that Washington give us aid. If we get enough signatures on that petition it might mean something to them, since every name on that petition could mean a lost vote. You won't find anybody in Enid or Pond Creek who won't sign it. I'll draw it up tonight, Arnold. When I get it ready, you can start here in Enid. I'll handle Pond Creek."

"How long's that going to take, Jason?"

"It won't be done for a couple of days, Arnold. Then we can depend on more delay in Congress. You can always figure on that."

"That's a sorry thing to hear," Budd said gloomily.

"If I could hurry it up, Arnold, I would. I'd better be getting back to Pond Creek."

April walked with him to the door. She looked up into his face and said, "Life never gets simple, does it, Jason?"

"Nope, but try and tell that to Derry. Right now, he's floating high."

"I've got the feeling everything will turn out all right, Jason. Even though I talked to Ida Belle just once, I liked her."

Jason bent his head to kiss her. "I wasn't thinking about Ida Belle. I was thinking of this railroad mess. I never thought the company itself could be so vindictive. I wonder if some individual is pushing the railroad's efforts because of his hatred for Enid and Pond Creek."

He shook his head. "No, that's not possible."

"Quit worrying about it, Jason. It'll turn out all right."

"You're more of an optimist than I am, April. Not only do we have to whip the Rock Island, we might wind up having to whip the government." He grinned bleakly. "That could be one hell of a job."

April stretched on tiptoes to kiss him again. "Just don't you get too involved."

Jason smiled. "You're remembering the time I was arrested for my part in taking up those tracks. I haven't forgotten it. I wasn't actually in jail, but close enough for me to smell that cell. I'll keep on working against the railroad, but I'll stay within the law. Good night, April."

CHAPTER FOURTEEN

Jason thought carefully about the wording of the petition for the next couple of days, then his pen moved rapidly. First, it demanded that legislation compel the railroad to recognize the county-seat towns as such. Next, that the railroad erect depots and stop on regular schedules. He leaned back and grinned twistedly. Now it all depended on how many signatures he obtained.

He decided to try Brown's saloon as his first stop, just as Sam Turner came down the street. "Sam!" he exclaimed. "Just the man I want to see. Come on in and I'll buy you a drink."

"Not in that place," Turner said stiffly. "Too many young punks hang out in there." He colored under Jason's measuring eyes, and he bristled. "Nobody laughs at Sam Turner."

"Is it that bad, Sam?"

"Bad enough that I'm spending my time in Enid. People listen to a man there."

"That depends on what a man talks about, Sam. Some subjects can get a man jailed."

"So you still got your tail tucked under, too," Turner sneered.

"I'm fighting the railroad as hard as you are," Jason said, his voice hardening.

"You sure haven't shown it," Turner scoffed.

Jason thrust the first sheet of the petition toward Turner. "Maybe this will change your mind. It's a petition to Congress to make them turn against the Rock Island. I thought you'd like to be the first to sign it."

Turner read the petition, his manner suspicious.

Jason tried to keep his exasperation from showing. "Damn it, Sam, isn't that what you want? To have the railroad build depots in Enid and Pond Creek and stop here on regular schedules?"

"That's what I want," Turner said in grudging admission. "But it won't happen if we stay on our knees, licking their hands."

"It won't happen by violence either, Sam. Every new instance of it only stiffens the Rock Island's attitude."

Turner stubbornly shook his head. "It won't do any good."

Jason's patience wore thin. "Oh, damn it, Sam. If you don't want to sign it, it's all right with me. But I'll tell you one thing. You'll be the only man in town who doesn't sign. That will tear you down a little more."

He turned to enter the saloon, and Turner grabbed his arm. "I'll sign it," he growled.

Jason nodded approvingly. "That's good, Sam. We're all in this fight together."

Turner's sniff said he still thought the petition was worthless.

Jason entered the saloon. Brown was doing a rushing business, for the place was packed. Jason's raised voice gained him attention. "Gather around, boys. This could be important." He explained what the petition was. "It's another way of putting pressure on Congress. The more signatures I collect, the more we bear down on our lawmakers."

"Do you think it will work, Jason?" a man called.

"I can't promise you it will," Jason replied. "But what have we got to lose? It's not going to cost you much effort, is it?"

"Hell no," several of them shouted. They almost trampled each other in the rush to sign. Not a man in the room refused, and Jason looked at the filled page of signatures with satisfaction. It was going well, but this was only a start.

It took him three days to cover the town. When he got to Enid, Budd was bubbling with enthusiasm. He, too, had collected every signature in town. "Even old Evans Deacon," he said soberly. "Evans was sorely sick. I started to pass up his house, but his wife insisted that I see him. I had to steady his hand while he signed. He died a couple of hours later, but he'd gotten in his last lick at the railroad. God, I wonder if the Rock Island knows how badly it's hated."

"If they don't, they'll learn," Jason said briefly.

"Have you heard what's developing?" Budd

asked. "Councilman W. R. Gregg of Enid, myself, and Mayor Wasson of Pond Creek are going to Washington as delegates. We're hoping that our pressure will help pass a bill that will force any railroad operating in the territory to establish and maintain passenger stations and freight depots at all established town sites. Doesn't that come under the Interior Department?"

Jason frowned thoughtfully. "I think it does, Arnold, but don't let your impatience rush you. It'll take time before your petition comes up for a vote in the House. After that, there's the Senate. They'll be even tougher than the House. Quite a few former railroad lawyers are in the Senate. Their votes will automatically go for the Rock Island. Senator Joseph Blackburn of Kentucky was a prominent railroad lawyer before he became a full-time politician."

Budd looked dismayed at Jason's recounting of the obstacles facing the small committee. "Jason," he begged, "why don't you come with us? You know your way around a lot better than any of us."

Jason shook his head. "I can't possibly get away now, Arnold. You'll do fine. Just don't let some slick-tongued congressman anger you. You can't outtalk them. They've already polished that ability in their campaign to get elected. You just keep your head." He tapped the thick sheaf of signed pages. "This backs up your right to be in

Washington. I've got a hunch that this time we're going to make progress."

Budd smiled wanly. "I sure hope you're right, Jason."

A few weeks later, Jason was at the depot to see the three men off. They had had to journey to North Enid to catch the train. He shook hands all around. "If something comes up and you need my advice, just wire me. Good luck, gentlemen."

He stood on the platform watching the train diminish in size as it sped away. He felt lost and lonely. He could well imagine how those three men on the train felt. They were up against an incredibly complex system, and they knew it. "Good luck," Jason muttered and buttoned up his overcoat. Winter was almost upon them, and the wind at this time of the year was sharp and biting. Jason prayed that the small committee wouldn't find Congress's attitude as chilling.

Jason got up from his desk and chucked a few logs into the already blazing stove. It took a lot of firewood to keep this little room bearable. He stood a moment longer, briskly rubbing his hands. Darkness came early, and the cold intensified until everyone longed for the approach of spring. He had just received a telegram, and his eyes scanned the message again:

Good news, Jason. The House passed bill 3603. It requires that all railroad companies operating lines through the territories of the United States over a right-of-way obtained under grant or act of Congress shall establish and maintain passenger stations and freight depots at all town sites established in said territories on the line of said railroad by authority of the Interior Department. The House of Representatives passed the bill almost unanimously, but we're meeting opposition in the Senate. Blackburn has been the stumbling block. He proposed that the Senate insist upon county seats that were permanently located. The House disagreed, and the bill went to conference. There it stands. There is talk that a Senate committee visit the two towns in question to see how bad they really need depot facilities. That's about it, Jason.

"I was afraid of that, Arnold," Jason muttered. "The two houses can kick it back and forth until you're thoroughly worn out." He looked up as the door opened, letting in a blast of icy air.

Derry came in, beating his arms across his body. "Cold enough to freeze a brass monkey," he said. "How much longer do you think it will last, Jason?"

"I'd say a safe bet would be spring. This kind

of weather makes a man appreciate spring and summer that much more."

Derry backed up to the stove and lifted his coattails. "Any news, Jason?"

"Not too good, I'm afraid. As usual, the Senate is wrangling over the railroad and the towns."

Derry's face fell. "That's too bad. Do you think the towns could lose out completely?"

"It's entirely possible," Jason said bitterly. "Until this country realizes that it cannot allow too much power to be gathered by one corporation, we will be in constant trouble. I'm afraid I haven't got a favorable opinion of our lawmakers' intelligence. Raw power and money have too much influence on them."

Derry crossed to a chair and sat down, staring fixedly at a wall.

He looked so troubled that Jason forgot his present problems. "What's eating on you, Clements?"

Derry gave him a twisted half-smile. "Does it show that much?"

"It does. Why don't you get it out?"

"You know I've been seeing a lot of Ida Belle?"

"I kinda guessed at it," Jason said dryly.

"Would it shock you if I told you I'm going to ask her to marry me?"

It might surprise Jason, but it wouldn't shock him. Derry was old enough to be sure of what he wanted.

"What does she think about this?" Jason asked cautiously.

That didn't move Derry's eyes from the wall. "I haven't discussed it with her yet." For the first time he turned his head and looked squarely at Jason. "Damn it, Jason, I want to get her out of that saloon."

"What if she likes it there?"

Derry glared at him so fiercely that Jason was sorry he said that. "She doesn't," he shouted. "I know it." He was silent for a long moment, and his expression was tormented. "You just don't know her background. She's been on her own ever since she was a small girl. Her parents died before she really had a chance to know them. She had to take anything she could find to make a living. She didn't have a chance to know anything different."

"I'm not arguing with you, Clements. Every man has the right to go after what he wants."

He stopped for so long that Derry said heatedly, "Go ahead, say it."

"I was just thinking it could be a rough road ahead for you. Some people won't accept her. You realize that?"

Derry's expression turned savage. "Anybody that causes her trouble has me to whip."

Jason sighed. Derry meant that, but it wouldn't change a thing. People could be essentially cruel. "It's your decision, Clements," he said softly. If

Ida Belle said yes, Jason could see a lot of hell ahead for Derry. Oh well, it was none of his busiess. He turned back to rereading Budd's telegram.

Derry was shaking inwardly as he entered the Palace Saloon. He knew Ida Belle liked him, but what if she hooted at his proposal? Oh God, he thought, it could happen.

Ida Belle was at the bar. She turned, saw him, and hurried toward him, a big smile on her face. She extended her hands, and Derry clasped both of them.

"If you knew how much I've missed you," Derry said.

"I've missed you too, Clements."

He shook his head. "This miserable weather has tied me in."

She nodded. "It's kept our business down, too. Have you been busy?"

"Jason has kept me hopping." He looked around helplessly. Oh God, so many people were within earshot. He had to talk to her in private. "Couldn't we take a table, Ida Belle?" he begged. If it had been his own choice, he would have picked a more glamorous place to propose to her, but right now he would take any place he could get. He waited until she sat down before he sat across from her.

"I guess the only solution is for you to move to Enid," Ida Belle smiled.

"I've been thinking of it," he said seriously. "Just as soon as I finish reading law with Jason."

"Does Jason think you will be a good lawyer?"

Derry groaned inwardly. Why were they on subjects that weren't important at the moment? "He thinks I will. Sometimes I think he's kinda proud of me. I've heard him say I can be a good lawyer if I don't let the thought of quick money turn my head."

"What does that mean?" she asked, puzzled.

"Usually to get quick money a man has to be dishonest somewhere along the line. Jason hammers on that all the time."

"You're not thinking of making quick money, are you?"

There would never be a better time to bring up the subject so important to him. He gulped, and the words poured out: "I'm thinking of the day we get married."

She stiffened, and her face went rigid. "What's that supposed to mean?" she cried.

He laughed, happiness radiating from his eyes. "You can understand better than that. Ida Belle, I'm asking you to marry me."

She shook her head violently. "That's impossible," she said frozenly.

"I thought you cared for me!"

"I do, I do." She ran the words together. "That's not the problem."

"Suppose you tell me what it is," he said half-angrily.

"I'm older than you are, Clements."

"Four years," he scoffed. "That's nothing."

Ida Belle briefly closed her eyes. When she opened them again he saw the pain. "It's everything," she said, her voice determined.

"I guess I'm the thick one now. I don't understand." He reached for her hand lying on the table, but she evaded him. His eyes darkened; maybe he had been fooling himself into thinking she cared for him.

She saw the pain touching his eyes and said quickly, "It's my background, Clements. I'm a saloon girl."

"Do you think that's important to me?"

"Maybe not," she answered. "But it could matter to other people. Think of your future. It could be ruined. People would point at you. If they didn't actually say anything, you'd know it was in their minds."

"I'd knock their damned heads off," Derry flared. "Are you afraid of that possible talk?"

"Not for myself," she assured him. "Only for you."

"Let me tend to that worry," Derry said slowly. "Ida Belle, I'm asking you again to marry me. I love you. What can I do to prove it to you?"

Her eyes caressed his face. "You already have. I don't need any more proof."

"Then you don't love me," he said, his tone anguished.

She almost reached out to stop his words. "Don't ever say anything like that again, Clements."

He frowned at her. "What's your real reason?"

"Clements," she wailed, "compared to you, I'm an uneducated woman. I would only drag you down."

"What nonsense," he said, elation lighting his face. "Now that that's all settled, will you think about it?" he begged.

Ida Belle held her head and rocked back and forth. "You're driving me crazy," she moaned. "Do we have to talk about it any more?"

A broad smile spread across Derry's face. He was winning; he felt it. "We won't talk about it any more if you promise to think about it." He stared in disbelief. She was shaking her head.

"Clements, why can't we just keep on like this? Nothing would have to change."

He stubbornly shook his head. "Because I want you for my wife."

"It won't work, Clements," she said faintly.

She was beginning to yield. He sensed it. "It will," he said. "I know it will."

"Oh, Clements," she said brokenly. "You drive me crazy."

"I will until you say yes," he said. "We won't talk about it any more tonight. But I'll be thinking about it. Every time you look at me, you'll know what I'm thinking."

CHAPTER FIFTEEN

Derry wasn't there when Jason opened the office in the morning. He must be having one hell of a night, Jason thought. Ida Belle must have said yes. With that answer, all thoughts of other times and places would fade from Derry's mind.

Another telegram had been delivered to him, and he opened it with an eerie feeling of disaster. "The Senate is stalling," Budd wired. "We're returning to fight it through the courts from that end."

Jason laid the telegram down, his eyes shadowed. "You won't find it any easier going here, Arnold," he muttered.

Derry came in, his face beaming. He was in the highest spirits, not even complaining about the weather.

Jason glanced at the clock. "You must be planning on becoming a banker instead of a lawyer," he commented.

"Nothing you can say will bother me today," Derry said blissfully.

"Something happen last night you want to tell me about?"

Derry winked. "Not just everything, but I asked Ida Belle to marry me."

Evidently, she didn't turn him down, or he

wouldn't be in these high, good spirits. "And she said yes?" Jason asked in mild astonishment. Ida Belle was a practical woman. He hadn't expected her to agree to such a harebrained scheme.

"Oh, she protested, all right, Jason. She came up with every pretext she could think of."

"And that makes you happy?"

Derry shook his head. "It was her reasons for not wanting to marry me that were the big problem. But she promised to think about it. That's the first big step, isn't it?"

Jason shook his head in amazement. Derry was a more persuasive man than he thought. He must have used pure logic. It looked as though he had picked the right profession. "I'm glad for you, Clements. And I hope it turns out just the way you want." But there was a big gap between Ida Belle agreeing to think about marrying Derry and her actually agreeing to marry him. What if her final decision is against him? Oh Lord, no. That would shatter Derry. "Keep pressing her," he advised. "The more time you give her to make up her mind, the more likely her decision is to be against you."

"I'll keep pushing," Derry said solemnly. "Where are you going?"

Jason was putting on his overcoat. "To see April. I just received a telegram from her father. She will want to know when Arnold is coming home." Jason chuckled. "Budd has a frugal mind. He wouldn't spend money on two telegrams when one will do." He paused at the door. "Keep in mind what I advised you about Ida Belle."

"I will," Derry promised.

Jason kept thinking about the wire as he rode toward Enid. He wondered if the news would sink the townspeople into a deadening apathy or arouse them to anger that would break out into violence. He would bet on violence.

April admitted him at his knock. "Come in," she cried, "before you freeze to death."

"I kept warm thinking about you," he said and laughed.

"Brrr," she said, shivering. "You don't feel very warm."

"Then it's up to you to furnish the heat."

She slipped out of his arms. "You're getting awful. What will you be like a few months from now?"

Jason laughed in delight. "Better, I hope. I talked to Derry before I left the office. He's asked Ida Belle to marry him."

April's eyes grew bright with interest. Jason had noticed that that was the one subject that could fix and hold a woman's attention: talking about another woman's love life. "What did she say?"

Jason cocked an eyebrow. "She's thinking

about it. I hope it doesn't take her too long. Derry will die of impatience."

April made a face at him. "That's all you men think of."

"Women do, too. It makes for an interesting life."

She shook her head. "You're terrible."

He tried to catch her wrist, and she evaded his hand. "April, when will we get married?"

She gave him a secretive smile. "When Ida Belle gets serious, then maybe I'll consider it."

"That could be a long time or never," he howled in indignation.

"You'd better push Ida Belle as hard as you can." Then her face turned serious. "I wonder how things will turn out for them. Women can be pretty catty. With Ida Belle's background, they'll have a lot of material." Her eyes flashed. "Men can be equally cruel."

Jason thought how her outrage had risen when she first learned of Ida Belle. That had vanished when she was firmly convinced that Ida Belle was no longer a threat to her. "They'll have to work out their own problems," he grumbled. "The one I've got is about as much as I can handle."

She came over to him and traced a forefinger down the length of his nose. "Poor darling with all his problems. I'll go make some tea. At least you won't be cold."

Jason sat there, a smile broadening on his

face. Both of them knew how this courtship was going to turn out. It was only a matter of waiting for the proper time to arrive. He stirred restlessly. The waiting was the hardest thing to face.

Jason heard the singing of the teakettle. He hadn't said a thing about her father, and that was his reason for coming over.

April came back, carrying a tray loaded with the teapot and cups. She poured the tea and asked, "Sugar?"

He nodded. "You know how I like it."

She ladled in two teaspoons. "Just like Papa likes it." Her face was touched with concern. "I wonder how he's getting along. It's been so long since I've heard from him. He's completely thrown himself into this railroad fight. I wish it was over."

Jason nodded. "Everybody involved feels the same way. As a matter of fact, I heard from Arnold this morning. That's why I came over."

She frowned at him. "I thought it was because of me." She sighed. "A woman can be so gullible."

Jason laughed with genuine amusement. "We males are lucky they are. Arnold wired that he's returning to Enid next Thursday."

April studied him. "Isn't that unexpected? The last letter I received from him, he thought he'd be in Washington much longer."

Jason shook his head. "Things got snarled up in the Senate. I suspect Arnold took a pretty good licking. He wants to come home to lick his wounds and regroup."

"Poor Papa," she said sorrowfully. "Jason, will it ever end?"

"Right now it doesn't look like it. I'll rent a carryall next Thursday and come by to pick you up. Is that all right?"

She nodded her agreement. "I am anxious to see him."

"I want to see him too. Perhaps things aren't as bleak as his telegram sounds."

"You'll stay for supper, Jason?"

"I'd like to, but this leaves me a lot of work to clear up."

April walked to the door with him. "If I didn't know better, I'd think you're seeking an excuse to avoid spending more time with me."

He hugged her tight and chuckled. "One of these days, you're going to eat those words."

"I'll be waiting for that," she challenged.

Jason was still laughing as he mounted. He waved to her and turned for Pond Creek. That was some gal.

The wind howled across the bleak prairie as Jason and April waited inside the depot. It sought every crevice in the building and filled the small room with the cold air.

Jason glanced at the Seth Thomas clock on the wall. "Wouldn't you know the damned railroad would pick a day like this to be late?" He impatiently paced the area before the large glass window. "It's more than an hour now."

"I'm thinking more of that poor horse out in this cold," April murmured.

"I left him and the carryall back of the depot. That will cut off most of the wind. He'll probably get along better than we're doing."

A porter shuffled by, and Jason asked, "Why don't you throw a couple of chunks of wood in the stove?"

The porter shrugged. "It wouldn't do any good. At this time of year, this room gets bitter cold and there's nothing you can do about it." He looked at Jason's frown and sighed. "All right, if you insist. But you'll see. It won't get any warmer." He filled the stove and ambled away.

"April, you go and stand near the stove. I want to be where I can see the train coming."

She started to refuse, but the cold got to her, for she nodded weakly. "All right, Jason."

He stayed at the window, glancing back at April every now and then. Finally his head lifted as he thought he heard the faraway wail of an engine's whistle. He turned to April and waved for her to join him. He held her inside the depot. "Wait until the train stops, April."

Budd, Gregg, and Wasson looked more beaten than the trip alone could have caused. Not just beaten, Jason thought; they looked crushed. They shook hands all around and exchanged a few words. Budd spent a few seconds hugging and kissing his daughter.

"Good trip?" Jason asked.

"A rotten trip," Wasson said. "I mean it. I believe hell is peopled with politicians. Of all the backbiting, self-seeking people—" He broke off and shook his head.

"I've got a carryall back of the depot," Jason said. "Let's get out of this wind." He saw to the stowing of the luggage and climbed in. Wasson sat next to him, and Jason appreciated that. He snapped the reins at the horse, and it welcomed the chance to move. At least, the pace got the blood circulating.

"You were saying something about politicians," Jason prompted.

"I didn't say nearly enough," Wasson said grimly. "That damned Senate blocked us every way we turned. Mostly due to those ex-railroad lawyers."

"You think it's hopeless, then?"

"I didn't say that," the mayor corrected. "But so nearly that it approaches the hopeless. I tried to get help from some of the wiser heads, but their advice was to go through the courts. Enid and Pond Creek now have to bring a mandamus to compel the railroad to put in depots and sidetracks in their corporate limits."

"Do we have a chance of winning?"

"Possibly," Wasson said glumly. "But the worst is the time it'll take. The Territorial Supreme Court doesn't convene at Guthrie until June 18. Justices Dale and Bierer will be among those on the bench."

"Honest justices?"

"Maybe," Wasson said cautiously. "I don't think they've been up against anything as powerful as the railroad. You can bet the Rock Island will have its smartest people on the case. All we can do is to wait and see how the court decision comes out. We've also got to see that the hotheads are contained. The wrong move before the trial will hurt us."

Jason stared out over the rump of the horse. "That's going to be hard to do."

Wasson's bobbing head agreed. "Those damned railroad lawyers will use any act of violence against the Rock Island to bolster their case. We don't want to lose before we even step into court."

"No," Jason agreed. He was silent, thinking of all the work ahead.

Wasson must have guessed his thoughts, for he said, "Jason, don't you have a good student reading law with you?"

"He is at that," Jason said proudly. "Maybe he's so good because his teacher is so good."

Wasson slashed the air with the edge of his palm, dismissing Jason's feeble witticism. "Can you hire him right now? You're going to need help and lots of it."

Jason thought about it briefly. "I think Derry can go out on his own now. All right, I'll hire him." He wasn't happy about it, for money wasn't too plentiful. But, on the favorable side, it would let him keep a close eye on Derry and Ida Belle. And, he would need help with his work. He would pay Derry the best salary he could afford and hope to skid by.

Chapter Sixteen

The frigid months slipped into spring, and the pressure never slackened. Jason didn't know there was so much paperwork readying a case to be presented before a Territorial Supreme Court. He kept Derry jumping, and he had never seen him happier.

"Ida Belle's bending," Derry announced elatedly. "My getting a regular job has its influence. Jason, I think ultimately she will say yes."

"Good," Jason said abstractedly. He had to check and recheck every line of his presentation. He couldn't afford a slipup this close to the trial date.

"Do you think we can get this through, Jason?"

"It wouldn't be the safest bet in the world, but we'll go in and raise all the hell we can."

As it turned out, Jason didn't get a chance to raise any hell at all. The first thing the Rock Island attorneys did was demand a full bench before answering the writ or making an argument. The hearing was delayed pending the appearance of Judge Scott, who was holding court in Pottawatomie County. When Scott joined the Supreme Court bench, the railroad refused to file an answer immediately.

When court finally convened, the silver-haired senior railroad lawyer demanded that the bench squash the case, which the bench overruled. The half-dozen railroad lawyers conferred briefly, then refused to argue the case until Judge McAtee joined the bench. The silver-haired lawyer looked over at Jason and smiled. Jason writhed under the condescension in that smile. These canny lawyers were whipping him six ways from the deuce, and Jason couldn't even pick up a card.

The railroad man asked for permission to approach the bench, and it was granted. He asked for an adjournment, claiming the railroad couldn't get witnesses in time for this session. He also asked for a jury. The court agreed to adjourn the case until the next sitting in August.

Jason and Derry left the courtroom, their faces blank masks. "Is that what we're going to be up against from here on?" Derry asked. "I feel like I've been beaten and wasn't given a chance to swing a blow in return."

"That's it, all right," Jason said flatly. "Wait until the newspaper gets hold of this."

Indeed, Isenberg's *Wave* was as strident as ever:

We have seen nothing but a dodge to gain time. The machine has slipped a cog. When August comes, the machinery will throw a half-dozen cogs, for the court will

195

conclude it is too hot to try the case. If the citizens want justice, it looks as though they'll again have to take matters into their own hands.

Jason crumpled up the copy of the *Wave* and flung it savagely across the room. "That tears the lid off of hell," he announced. The railroad might deny vehemently that the last thing it wanted was bloodshed, but every maneuver it pulled was another shove in that direction.

Sam Turner read the *Wave* too. It sent him into a tearing rage, only confirming what he had believed all along. "I wonder what Jason thinks about all this now," he muttered. "He thinks he's so damned smart."

Turner's determination to do something against the railroad hadn't weakened, but he wasn't going to try and do anything in Pond Creek. They'd already shown him what they thought of him. They had pushed their heads deep into the sand, and they didn't dare raise them enough to take a small peek. All because they had been arrested once. Hell, that hadn't even cost them any time, but they were still running scared.

Enid would be the place to stage any coming events. There was a younger group over there filled with a wild deviltry. Turner was sure that group had devoured the newspaper and would be primed to try anything. All they needed was a gentle shove in the right direction and some sage advice.

He saw groups of people congregated on the corners, and he didn't have to guess what they were talking about. Everybody had read the latest article, and if the paper hadn't given sufficient coverage, tongues alone had a powerful and far-reaching effect.

Turner stopped at the largest saloon in Enid, dismounted, and sauntered inside. This wasn't a usual night. The place was packed with customers, but most of them were grouped around one table. Turner couldn't see the speaker, but he had a commanding voice, carrying plainly to all corners of the room. Most of these men knew Turner, and his pushing toward the center of the crowd didn't arouse much resentment.

Bill Cawson was the speaker, and that didn't surprise Sam. Cawson was a fire-eater, too young for experience to have taught him much. "How much longer are we going to stand for this?" he bawled. "That blasted Rock Island is making us look like fools! If we don't like it, who cares?"

"I care!" a dozen voices rang out. "It's time we do something! It's plain that the courts aren't going to act."

Cawson looked around. "Anybody got any suggestions?" He saw Turner and shouted. "Here's somebody who might be able to tell us what to do. He ramrodded the derailing of the train in Pond Creek."

That wasn't quite true. Jason was the one who came up with that suggestion, but Turner wasn't turning down any credit that accrued from that incident. He had their attention, and he had no intention of losing it. "That wasn't such a good idea," he said and grimaced. "It got a lot of the boys arrested. All it did was force the railroad to guard its track. I've done more thinking about it, and I've got a better idea. The track around Enid ain't being guarded. We can do almost anything we want there."

Eager men leaned toward him, their eyes shining. "You mean derail another train?"

They were turning toward him, and Turner was reveling in his leadership. Back in Pond Creek, folks hardly spoke to him. "Not that," he said. "It's too much work for the little results we got. I've got to do some more thinking about this."

He had an idea full-blown in his head, but he didn't want to speak of it now, not with so many strangers here. If there was an informer present, he could run straight to the railroad. "We'll talk about it some more tomorrow," he finished.

"Hell," one of them said, "we're looking for action tonight."

"Not with me," Turner said, grinning wickedly.

The crowd hung around for a few more

minutes, then slowly drifted away. Only Cawson, Beacon, and Still were left. Cawson studied Turner and said, "You old coot. You've got something in mind. If I didn't smell it, I could see it shining out of your eyes."

"I didn't know all of that crowd," Turner said affably. "I know you three. I know that anything we talk about here won't get no further."

Cawson sucked in a breath, making a queer whistling sound. "I knew it," he exclaimed. "I knew there was something kicking around in that head."

"Besides, we don't need a crowd," Turner said. "All that would do is attract attention. The four of us can do what I've got in mind."

"What's this plan you're so proud of?" Cawson asked.

Turner looked around surreptitiously, then leaned across the table and lowered his voice. "What I've got in mind will hit the Rock Island where it hurts. I plan to wreck an entire train."

The others' eyes widened in awe at the magnitude of Turner's plans.

"Would you use dynamite?" Cawson asked breathlessly.

Turner scowled at him. "What would I want that stuff for?"

"To blow up the tracks. That's the fastest way I know of."

"Naw." Turner shook his head in disgust. "I'm

going to let that train wreck itself." He paused, looking highly pleased with himself.

"For God's sake," Cawson begged, "will you get on with it?"

"Do you know that bridge across the dry creek about a mile south of Enid?"

"Ah," Cawson said in sudden enlightenment. "You're going to blow up that bridge?"

"Nothing that crude. Can you get a couple of crosscut saws?" At Cawson's nod he went on. "Meet me at the bridge at one o'clock in the morning. There won't be anybody around to watch what we're doing."

Cawson and the other two begged for more details, but Turner kept shaking his head. "Just be at that bridge," he commanded.

Turner left the saloon fifteen minutes later. Several men called to him as he passed, but their voices weren't very cordial. They might be disdainful now, since the old man hadn't disclosed any startling news. But wait until tomorrow morning. He could almost taste the reaction of Enid as he thought of the earth-shattering news that would hit it. One Rock Island train would be completely wiped out, and only with the simple use of crosscut saws. Turner could already savor his elation at the thought of seeing a train wreck at the bridge. How those stupid bastards in Pond Creek would wish they'd joined him when they heard the news! They thought of him as a useless old man, did they? Well, he'd show them.

It was too dark for Turner to see the oncoming men, but he could hear them. They must be carrying the crosscut saws across their shoulders, for with each step the saws bent and rebounded with small musical notes.

He finally saw them, dark blobs against the background of the night. "Over here," he called.

Cawson and the other two joined him, and Cawson lowered his saw to the ground. "It's not heavy," he grumbled, "but they're hard to carry. They bounce with every step."

"You're going to love them before this work is over," Turner chortled.

"I won't if you don't tell us what you have in mind," Cawson grumbled.

Turner led them to the center truss of the bridge. The structure was mounted on eight-by-eight timbers, and it was going to take a lot of sawing to cut them through. "We'll do these five supports," Turner said. "Saw them on an angle with the lower side of the cut downhill. When the weight of the train rests on the bridge, it'll force the cut timbers to slip. We'll need to cut two more posts of the adjoining trusses north and south so that the bridge will swing its burden to the west. She'll tumble that way."

"My God," Cawson whispered, "you're a genius."

"Not quite," Turner disclaimed. "I want to hit the Rock Island such a blow that it'll hurt them for a long time. I studied some bridges, seeing where a few simple cuts would do the most harm. Now we'd better get to work."

The crosscuts were sharp, and for a long while there was only the muted buzzing as teeth bit into the timbers. Turner was on one end of the saw, Cawson handled the other. Turner had done a lot of crosscut work. A good saw man put all his strength into pushing the saw back to his co-worker, bearing down on the handle. Turner couldn't see a growing pile of sawdust, but that was all to the good. After they had finished here, no idle stroller would pass by and notice the evidence. And a steady breeze should disperse it even further.

Turner and Cawson had their timbers cut before the other sawmen were done. The bridge groaned and settled down in the tiny space of the cut, but its main support was still beneath it. Cawson jerked and flinched at the small wrenching sound, and his eyes rolled as he looked up at the bridge.

"It ain't coming down," Turner assured him. "It's only settling. But the train's weight will knock it enough out of line to make it collapse. How are you others coming?" he called softly.

"Almost through," one of them answered.

Turner inspected the timber they were working on. "Better than half through," he said in a wheezing voice. "Damn, but I'm out of breath. I'm not the man I once was."

"You're still a better man than I am," Cawson panted. "Jesus, my lungs are on fire."

"It'll pass," Turner said unfeelingly. A great elation was filling him.

"Just looking at it, one would think it's as steady as a rock," Cawson marveled when the whole job was done. "But the next train that attempts to cross will bring it down."

"You can bet on it," Turner said placidly. "Let's get these saws out of sight."

"Ain't we going to stay to see the wreck?" Cawson asked in disappointment.

"I wouldn't miss it," Turner replied. "If I've got the schedule right, there's a train due from the south at ten o'clock in the morning. We'll watch it from that small grove of trees on that hill. We'll come out here singly so it won't arouse too much curiosity."

"Do you really think it will work, Sam?" Cawson asked.

"Would you like to be riding that train?" Turner countered.

Cawson shut his eyes, visualizing all the cuts made in those sturdy timbers. "God, no," he said.

"That's your answer," Turner said, pleased. He turned and walked away, letting the other men carry the saws. They were a lot younger than he.

• • •

Sam approached the small grove of trees a half hour before ten o'clock. As early as he was, he was the last to arrive. The other three were already there, sprawled in the thin grass in the shade.

"You weren't very anxious, Sam," Cawson remarked.

Turner chuckled. He knew the fierce, young blood that coursed through those veins. "We've still got a time to wait. Usually these trains run behind schedule."

The minutes dragged away. Every now and then one of the men asked what time it was. Sam would pull out his watch and remark sardonically, "Two minutes since you asked me the last time. Quit fretting. The time will pass." Damn but this was the longest thirty minutes he had ever spent.

"You hear something?" Cawson asked as Turner raised his head from the ground.

"Thought I did. Guess not." He started to lower his head, then cocked an ear at the faint, reedy wail of an engine whistle. He sat bolt upright. "Didn't think my ears had gotten that bad," he growled. "The train's coming."

Everybody but Turner stood, and he said waspishly, "Why don't you wave your arms and yell? That'd be a sure way to warn the engineer."

They sat down, their faces sheepish. "Sorry, Sam," Cawson said. "We just got a little excited."

Turner's stern face didn't ease. "Hold your excitement until it's done." The engine whistled again, and he evaluated the nearness of the sound. "Should be in sight any second now." He waited another moment, then uttered a satisfied, "Ah. I thought so. Here it comes."

Nothing alerted the engineer to any possible trouble. He had full steam up on the engine, and it roared onto the bridge.

None of the watching men said anything, but Turner heard the collective breaths rattling in their throats.

The engine and four of its cars were on the bridge now, and nothing had happened. Turner couldn't swear to it, but he thought he saw the bridge sag under the train's weight. The engineer must have felt the bridge's giving, and he opened the throttle a notch wider. He had a little power left, for the engine seemed to lunge forward, dragging the first three cars after it.

Turner felt a catch in his breathing. After all his planning, was the train going to get safely across the bridge?

The rending and snapping of tortured timbers came first. The outside posts of the north and south trusses buckled, letting the bridge sag to the west. The crackling of the timbers grew louder, and suddenly the whole structure collapsed. The engine and three cars had made it safely across, and the weight of the following cars snapped the couplings. A giant hand was playing jackstraws with the freight cars, spilling them in the gully. Turner counted twelve wrecked units, some of them battered beyond recognition.

Three cars were loaded with lumber and six with wheat. The lumber cars were split open, and the wood was piled all along the gully, some of it so splintered that it was worthless for anything but toothpicks. Freshly harvested wheat gleamed in yellow piles, knee-deep from the spot where the cars first struck and continuing to where they finally stopped rolling. Two cars were loaded with empty beer kegs, and they were thrown all over. A lone tanker was battered completely out of shape. The caboose had tipped over just at the south approach of the bridge, and loud screams for help came from within.

"We'd better get out of here right now," Turner said.

Cawson shook his head. He was reveling in all this destruction. "I want to stare at it a little longer."

"When the railroad hears about this, they'll put every hound they've got on our trail. Those hounds will chew on our tails all the way to jail. Do you want that?"

Cawson swallowed hard. "Guess not," he muttered. "Come on, boys. Let's get going."

At every other step Cawson looked back. Turner knew how he felt. He knew the same impulses himself.

CHAPTER SEVENTEEN

The news of the wreck set Enid wild in celebration. Every place Turner went, he heard some new account of the wreck. One man said, "That'll show the bastards. I heard that the conductor and brakeman in the caboose were bruised all to hell. It served them right. You know how stuck-up those railroad employees are, particularly the conductors."

Turner nodded. He had swallowed enough of their haughty manners to make him want to vomit. "Anybody else get hurt?" he asked in a tight voice.

"Two tramps were stealing a ride in a carload of lumber. That car dropped into the deepest part of the gully. From what I heard, one of them was hurt badly, but they think he'll live. They're not sure about the other one. They must have been moaning like hell for the rescuers to have heard them."

Turner's jaw clenched tight. He hated to hear that about the tramps. He hadn't wanted to hurt anybody. He threw his self-accusations aside. The Rock Island had hurt far more people than a couple of tramps. What he did had to be done.

"You going out to the wreck?" the man asked.

Turner shook his head.

"You'll see quite a sight. Everybody in town is going. The hacks are full. They can hardly keep up with the rush."

"Maybe I'll go a little later," Turner muttered and broke away from the garrulous man. He walked down the street, his shoulders slumping. He didn't regret a thing, but the news about the tramps still bothered him. Being crushed in that lumber car must have created a lot of suffering.

"Sam, hold on," a voice called to him.

Turner wheeled as a hack pulled to his side of the street. He groaned at the sight of its passenger. He didn't want to talk to Jason Keeler right now.

"Sam, what are you doing in Enid?" Jason greeted him. "I'm on my way to the wreck. I want to see how bad it is. Climb in. I'll take you out."

Turner wouldn't look up from the ground. "I'm not interested in any train wreck," he said in a surly tone.

Jason studied him, and his eyes sharpened. Something was bothering Turner, and he speculated upon it being connected with the wreck. "I wondered what you were doing in Enid, Sam. Did you come over here for some particular reason?"

Turner flashed him an indignant look. "What's that supposed to mean?"

"I'll put it plainer, Sam. Did you have anything to do with wrecking that train?"

"What makes you say that?" Turner spluttered.

"I know of your hatred for the Rock Island. I think you'd do anything to get what you call even. You may have gone too far this time, Sam. The Rock Island will use every means at its hands, and believe me they've got plenty, to find the culprit. You're going to need God's help if they find out you're the one they want."

That scared Turner, and he tried to cover it with a false bravado. "What are you going to do, run to them and babble your guts out? It'd make you a big man with the Rock Island."

Jason sighed. "You know me better than that, Sam. We were friends not so long ago."

"It sure don't sound like it now," Turner growled.

Jason's face was set in hard lines. "I pray you didn't have anything to do with it, Sam. Not only because of this wreck, but because of the bad example it sets. Other hotheads will hear of your success, and they'll use the same method or a variation of it. You've opened the door to an actual war, Sam. Now the Rock Island can scream to the government, demanding protection. And the government will send it. We'll see soldiers down here before this is all over. Enid and Pond Creek will lose all chance to settle this matter peacefully, all because of your desire to get even with the railroad."

"Will you shut up?" Turner screamed. He'd had

more than enough of Jason's accusations. "You haven't got a bit of proof. All you've got is guesses." He turned and stumbled blindly down the street.

Jason shook his head as he watched Turner go. There was no doubt in his mind that Sam was involved in that wreck. Just how much, he didn't know.

The hack driver had been listening curiously. "Do you think he had something to do with it?"

"I never accused him of that," Jason said quietly. "I was only trying to keep another citizen from losing his head."

The driver shrugged, unconvinced. "Hell, you sure sounded like it." A thought occurred to him, and he exclaimed, "Say! I'll bet the railroad would pay a good reward for the name of the guilty one."

Jason knew an instant alarm for Turner. If this driver went to the railroad officials and told them what he had heard, those officials would hound Sam until they penned and broke him. By an average life-span, Turner didn't have a lot of years remaining. Jason certainly didn't want him spending those few years in a jail.

"You've been out to the wreck scene?" Jason asked.

"Four times this morning," the driver boasted.

"It took a powerful man to cause it," Jason said.

"They used saws," the driver protested.

"Hah!" Jason said in triumph. "You say *they* used saws. You figure there was more than one?"

The driver nodded, his face cautious.

"If you were leading that bunch, would you have picked that old man to join you?"

The driver's eyes narrowed as he thought back. "I guess not," he said uncertainly. His voice strengthened. "Hell no, I wouldn't pick him. I'd be afraid he'd fall on his face at any moment."

Jason nodded complacently. "Then you see why I don't go to the railroad officials myself and point them in the old man's direction."

The driver grinned. "It would make you look pretty foolish."

"It would," Jason said with conviction.

All the way to the collapsed bridge, he thought of Sam Turner. He wasn't as feeble as Jason made him out to be, and he had that hellish determination driving him. If this was Jason's railroad, and he had this much evidence pointing Turner's way, Jason would pounce on him before the day was over. He was glad he had talked any suspicion out of this driver's mind, but he'd better keep a close eye on Turner. Sam had already done enough harm.

Hacks were lined up on both sides of the bridge. People clambered into the gully for a closer look at the damage. A few of the braver ones had ventured out onto the remaining edges.

Jason wasn't that foolhardy. He climbed down into the gully, and one man asked, "Your first look at it?"

Jason nodded.

"I been here since right after it happened," the man boasted. "I saw them take the brakeman and conductor out of the caboose. They were busted up pretty bad. I saw them bring out the tramps, too. One of them was screaming. I guess he hurt something awful. The other one was unconscious."

My God, Jason thought. The morbid fascination a disaster had for people.

"The railroad will be glad those tramps got hurt," the man continued.

"Why's that?"

The man grinned viciously. "Those tramps were stealing a ride off the Rock Island. They needed to be punished."

Jason shook his head. The people around here had a hatred for the railroad that was worse than a disease. "What will you think when the railroad appeals to the government and the government sends soldiers? All the local law will have to stand against this sort of thing."

The man's eyes gleamed like hot coals. "I've got a gun. I'll fight the bastards. I won't be alone, either."

Jason turned and began to climb up to where his hack waited. It was useless trying to talk to men of this caliber. They were consumed by a madness, and nothing would erase the coming violence and bloodshed.

Jason wished he had stopped at the Budd house before he went out to the railroad wreck. Seeing it had left him feeling totally depressed.

April answered his knock. After a kiss, she studied his expression. "Something bad has happened. I can tell by the way you look."

Jason managed a grimace. "That bad, huh? I went out to see the destroyed bridge. Have you seen it?"

April shuddered. "I had the chance. I don't need something like that to make me feel worse. What do you think is going to happen, Jason?"

"I think all hell is going to break loose," he said grimly. "Where's Arnold? Has he seen the wreck?"

April nodded. "He went out a few minutes after the reports came in. He came back with the same look on his face."

"Is he here now?"

"He was called down to his office just a few minutes ago. I think he should be back soon."

Jason settled down in a chair. He might as well be comfortable while he waited.

"Have you had breakfast?"

"I've eaten," Jason replied. If he didn't keep himself anchored in the chair, he would be pacing.

April guessed at part of the reason for his agitation. "Aren't Ida Belle and Clements getting along?"

"Not too well. I'm afraid Ida Belle is one stubborn gal. The gloom on Derry's face gets thicker every day. I don't know what's going to happen between those two."

"Somebody should talk to her," April suggested.

There was mockery in Jason's grin. "Have you ever tried to talk to a woman when she's made up her mind?"

April flushed. She caught the subtle allusion to the quarrel they'd had. "I still think she'd listen to another woman where she might turn a deaf ear toward anything a man says."

"You may be right," Jason admitted. "I've done all I can. I'm staying out of it."

He turned his head as the door opened. Budd came into the room, deep trouble riding his face. "You know what's happened, Jason?"

"I just came back from there. I saw the wrecked bridge."

"Not just *that* bridge," Budd said, his voice tragic. "I just got a report that two more bridges were blown up, one near Enid and the other one near Pond Creek. My reporter said the explosions were terrible, and the bridges are completely destroyed. Those bridges are thirty miles apart, and there's no way through service can be furnished. What will I do, Jason?"

"I'm damned if I know, Arnold. This tears everything wide open."

"They'll send in the soldiers," Budd wailed.

"Most likely," Jason agreed. "The only thing I can see is that you personally try and talk some sense into the people. Make them understand how futile fighting the Army will be. I'll get back to Pond Creek and try to do the same thing." He walked to the door, stopped there, and looked back. "We're really in a mess now." He waved and received a shaky smile from April. Budd didn't see his wave; his head was buried in his hands.

Jason made record time in getting back to Pond Creek. He went about town calling the most influential men into his office for a meeting. Thirty of them crowded into the room. He eyed them sternly before he said in a tight voice, "You've all heard what's happened."

That brought out a chorus of guffaws, and men slapped each other on the back.

Jason's disgust grew. They were like children, never looking beyond the present. "It won't be so funny when troops come in to quell what the Rock Island will call anarchy. Do you want to see your neighbors shot? It can happen."

He turned his head as the door opened. His

face went rigid. Turner was entering the office. Jason groaned inwardly. That's all he needed was to have Sam further enflaming these men.

"Yes, Sam?" His voice wasn't friendly. "What do you want?"

There was a kind of pleading in Turner's face that Jason didn't quite understand. "I heard about two more bridges being blown up," he said in a low voice. "I'm afraid somebody got the idea from the destruction of the first bridge. I guess I just realized what could happen."

Maybe Turner would never admit his guilt, but this was all the admission Jason needed. "What's on your mind, Sam?" he asked coldly.

"Do you think soldiers will be sent in?"

"You can bet on it," Jason snapped. "I saw after our first scrape with the railroad just how powerful the Rock Island is. That's when I backed off—not in my mind, but with any physical acts. I knew the railroad would counter, and it's a hell of a lot stronger than all of us combined with Enid's people. Before this is over, Enid and Pond Creek will look like occupied countries."

Eyes rolled uneasily, but the jut of stubborn jaws hadn't lessened. "Then we'll fight the soldiers!" somebody in the rear of the room yelled.

"Who said that?" Jason demanded sharply.

The culprit wouldn't identify himself, and

Jason was ready to blast them again when Turner said, "May I say something else, Jason?"

"I think you'd better," Jason said grimly.

Sam held up both hands to quell the murmur running through the crowd. "I know what all of you think of me," Turner said. His voice didn't tremble. "It doesn't matter. But what happens to Pond Creek does. It's my town, your town. I don't want to see anything bad happen to it. If the soldiers come in, some hotheaded fool like me is liable to lose all control and try to settle things his way. If one of those soldiers is hurt, can't you see what will happen? The soldiers will return the fire, and a lot of our neighbors will be killed. If you make them mad enough, they may burn down our buildings and houses. I don't want that. I don't think you do, either."

"You scared, Turner?" somebody taunted.

"You're damned right I am," Turner confessed. "I know I was guilty in trying to push the trouble forward. I see now where Jason was right. All this should be left up to the courts."

That brought him a crescendo of howls. A voice yelled, "They haven't done any good yet!"

"It takes patience for the courts to work," Jason said calmly. "Waiting is as important as getting in a fight. I want all of you to promise me you'll do nothing against the railroad."

A steady rumble of muted oaths ensued. Jason waited until they were out of the listeners' systems. "If you can't promise that, will you agree that we meet again and discuss this some more if things get worse?"

They gave Jason a reluctant agreement and slowly filed out. Turner was the last man to leave. His face was very sober as he said, "I meant everything I said, Jason."

"I know that, Sam," Jason said heartily. What Turner had said had turned the tide. "What made the big change in you?"

"I guess it was hearing about that one tramp. By his screaming, he musta been going through hell. He didn't have anything to do with what happened, yet I put him through that suffering. It ate on me pretty hard, Jason. Then I got to thinking that if the soldiers came there could be a lot more suffering, suffering by the people I used to call friends. That wouldn't let me sleep. Nothing's worth that, Jason."

Jason moved to Turner and draped an arm over his shoulders. "It takes a big man to see where he's wrong and admit it. I'm proud of you, Sam."

Turner blinked his eyes several times as though they stung. "It takes a long time for an old fool to get smart."

Jason laughed. "You're one of the lucky ones. Some men live out their lives and never reach that stage. I'd like to buy an old and valuable friend a drink. Are you accepting?"

A stiff grin moved Sam's lips. "I'm accepting." He paused as a new thought struck him. "All this current trouble started in Enid. Can it be stopped there?"

Jason's face was troubled. He didn't know how much influence Budd had on his constituents. Let him have a whole lot, he prayed. A whole lot.

CHAPTER EIGHTEEN

The soldiers came, and with them the arrival of hard times. The insolence of power infected them, and they swaggered about the streets, barking their obnoxious orders.

The destroyed bridges caused the Rock Island nothing but trouble. The morning trains exchanged passengers at the demolition sites, and cattle had to be sidetracked at Kremlin.

Jason didn't know how things were going in Enid. Better than Pond Creek, he prayed. He had wanted to go over to Enid to check, but trying to keep a firm hand on the seething lid in Pond Creek took every available minute.

Just seeing the soldiers on the street enraged the Enid people. Budd had ordered the soldiers to leave town within twenty-four hours of their arrival, and the insolent laughter of refusal only increased the citizens' fury.

A special train from Enid that carried the military approached South Pond Creek's limits, and two dynamite bombs exploded. One charge went off under the train, doing no damage. The other blew out a cattle guard and shattered a rail.

Deputy Marshal Madison was on that train with his posse. At the first opportunity he wired Brooks the details, adding that, "While not caring to meddle in territorial affairs, it looks to me as though it will be necessary at once to suspend sheriffs and other officers and replace them with men who will attend to their duty fearlessly. If there is any way by which it can be done lawfully, every house should be searched at once for dynamite."

Brooks paced his office while he considered his report. Olney had to know what Madison had wired. He sat down and scribbled rapidly:

Conditions are getting chaotic. A soldier was fired on in Enid. Luckily, the bullet missed, but it shows the extremes the towns are prepared to go through to fight back. The marshal was preparing to send an additional force of deputies to Enid and Pond Creek, and found the tracks mined with dynamite. Any citizen inclined to give information is threatened and intimidated. There are not enough soldiers to deter the mobs. I request that territorial authorities remove the sheriffs and other officers in the two towns and send military men to replace them and work earnestly at stopping the trouble.

He stared gloomily at the letter before he sealed it. He doubted it would be effective, but it took the load off his back.

April was standing at the window when she saw Ida Belle go by, carrying a valise. Some instinct warned her that Ida Belle was leaving Enid. She hurried out of the house and ran after the woman, calling, "Ida Belle, wait!"

Ida Belle finally heard her and slowly turned, her face defiant.

"Are you leaving town?" April asked.

"Yes," Ida Belle said shortly. "Trevlin kicked me out of the saloon. He said my wrangling with Clements was causing too much trouble."

"That's no reason," April said indignantly.

"I guess it was to him." Ida Belle tried to smile and failed. "I've got to get going, April. My hack's supposed to pick me up in a half hour."

"Where are you going?"

"To North Enid. There I'll catch a train to St. Louis."

April reached out and caught her arm. "Does Clements know about this?"

Ida Belle shrugged. "He came back last night. We had one hell of a quarrel. I told him I was leaving. We got in a shouting match. I guess that was when Slim got enough of it."

"Ida Belle, do you care for him?"

Her eyes shifted, then met April's firmly. "I do. But it wouldn't work."

"Why not? He cares for you."

"Because too many people know of my background. I tried to point out how it could hurt him. He wouldn't listen."

"You're putting too much importance on that background. Did you ever stop to think that it wasn't solely your fault? Life has a mean trick of pushing people into a corner. It's up to the individual to strike back."

Ida Belle was suffering. Her eyes were closed tightly, and her face was rigid. "People would always remember what I was, and they'd throw it in my face. I could stand that, but I'm not so sure about Clements. If I ever saw doubt on his face, I don't think I could bear it."

"You don't trust yourself or Clements very much, do you?" April asked softly.

Ida Belle doggedly shook her head. "I know what people think of me. I'm the girl who can be bought for a few drinks."

"I don't think that, Ida Belle."

"You've been nice," Ida Belle admitted, "but it wouldn't change anything."

April had a flash of inspiration. "Ida Belle, how would you and Clements like to be married in my house?"

"Mr. Budd is mayor of Enid," Ida Belle said dazedly. "He wouldn't allow it."

"Oh yes, he will," April retorted. "I'll invite some of the church members. They won't dare refuse because the mayor's daughter asked them."

That hard shell around Ida Belle was melting. April could see a few tears well up into her eyes. "Do you really think it would work?" Ida Belle asked breathlessly.

"Why don't you try it and see for yourself? Come in and wait until I get word to Clements. I'll get the preacher and make all the other arrangements. You're not going to pass up what could easily be the biggest day of your life."

"You really don't think I'd ruin Clements' future?" Ida Belle persisted.

"You've probably made it, Ida Belle. Don't you see? It's not what you've done in the past that's so important. It's what you do in the future."

"Oh God, I hope you're right," Ida Belle moaned.

April turned her back toward the house. "Trust me." She had a lot to do and not much time. First, she had to get the news to Clements and Jason and make some sort of wedding dress. Then there were arrangements to be made with the preacher, and a careful selection of guests. If she saw one look of disdain on anybody's face, she'd slap his head off.

Ida Belle was crying quietly by the time they reached the house. "Never a backward look,"

April counseled her. "From now on, you look ahead."

Ida Belle brushed the tears from her eyes. "You know, I'm beginning to believe what you say." Her head lifted and was carried proudly the last few steps to the door.

April squeezed her arm. "Clements can be a proud man."

The wedding was held in the afternoon two days later. The front room of the Budd house was packed until it was doubtful another guest could be admitted. Clements looked foolishly happy. He had bought a new suit, and the color suited him. April wondered if Jason had helped him select it. The Reverend Gleason stood at one end of the room, looking very solemn. He hadn't made a single protest when April asked him to marry Ida Belle and Clements. "Do you know her background, Reverend?" she had dared to ask him.

"I do," he'd said gently. "If all people were blamed for the past, it would really be a sorry world, wouldn't it?"

April went into the back room. Ida Belle had just finished dressing. The dress material was a lucky selection. Its blue sheen brought out the lovely shade of Ida Belle's eyes.

"Oh, April, I'm so scared," whispered the bride.

April patted her arm. "Don't be. I think you'll be pleasantly surprised." She led Ida Belle into the parlor, and she could feel the appreciation that ran through the guests' murmurs. Derry's face was so red April was afraid he would catch on fire. His eyes were glowing.

Ida Belle seemed to take strength from the sight of him. She managed a tremulous smile, went up to him, and clasped his arm with both hands.

Reverend Gleason started the ceremony. "Dearly beloved, we are gathered here—"

The rest of his words weren't clear to April. She was too intent on picking up the first jarring note that could mar the ceremony. But nothing like that was happening, she thought with a deep sense of relief. The nasty streak in humans had been wiped out for the moment. Here was only a man and woman being joined in wedlock.

"What God has joined together let no man put asunder," the reverend finished. "You can kiss your bride," he said to Derry.

Derry wrapped Ida Belle in his arms and kissed her long. There was no doubt that the past was dead for Ida Belle as she returned the kiss.

April glanced around the room. Every face was intent and soft. Something magic had touched everybody. Most of the women were crying. April couldn't blame them; her own eyes were moist.

Derry hustled his bride outside. A rented hack

was waiting. He helped Ida Belle up into it, both ducking a shower of rice. April stood beside Jason, watching the hack pull away. "It was a lovely wedding, wasn't it, Jason?"

"It was," he answered solemnly. "Something good touched all the people in that house."

"So you caught it, too?"

"How could I miss it?" he asked in mild surprise. "After all the strife and turmoil in Enid and Pond Creek, that sane moment was like a blessing. A half hour from now it may all be gone, but it was good while it lasted. I don't think a woman or a man felt like judging Ida Belle. It's just too bad it can't last forever."

Unconsciously, April seized his arm. "Where are they going?"

"Back to Pond Creek for a few days," Jason answered absently. "I talked to Clements after you told him Ida Belle had agreed to stay. He mentioned something about moving on to San Francisco. April, did watching all this change your mind?"

Her fingers pressed harder against his arm. "Yes," she said meekly. "Ask me when all this trouble is over and things settle back to normal."

Jason kissed her, regardless of how many people might see them. When he spoke his voice was husky. "Then I'd better work harder to see that it's settled soon."

CHAPTER NINETEEN

Sheriff R. H. Hager, County Attorney Daniels, and County Commissioner W. B. Cox were called to Guthrie on September 17 to answer for their failure to protect railroad property. Jason went along to give them what legal protection he could, and offer advice. The small group met an indignant Brooks.

Hager, a big gruff man, conferred briefly with Jason, then announced, "On the advice of our attorney, we will not resign."

"I can petition the Secretary of the Interior, Hoke Smith, to direct the governor to suspend or remove the sheriff and all deputies at Enid and Pond Creek," Brooks snapped.

"Then I suggest you go right ahead," Jason responded. He wasn't sure how solid the ground he stood on was; it all depended upon the Secretary's reaction.

"I'm wiring him immediately. You people stick around until I get the Secretary's answer," Brooks growled.

Jason nodded. "We'll be in the lobby of the Guthrie Hotel."

Brooks flung him a harassed look. "Just be damned sure you are."

The four men lounged in the hotel lobby. Their

boredom grew with the slow passage of time. Sheriff Hager said in a pleased tone, "One thing is sure. Some of the high muckamucks are getting worried."

"Don't count on that too much," Jason said. "We're a long way from home."

Most of the morning had passed before Brooks sent a clerk after them. "Mr. Brooks wants to see you right now."

"Ah," Jason said, "he's got an answer. Was it favorable or unfavorable?"

The clerk shrugged. "You better ask Mr. Brooks that, sir."

Brooks's jaw was rock-hard when the four men entered his office. Jason could barely keep his grin suppressed. "The answer wasn't to your liking?"

Brooks shoved a telegram toward Jason. "Read it for yourself," he said, his lips a thin angry line.

Jason's eyes lighted with interest as he picked up the telegram. He couldn't keep his grin from showing as he read.

In my opinion as Secretary, I believe that the exclusive jurisdiction to remove a sheriff from his office lies with the district court for the territory. The governor has wired President Ransom R. Cable of the Rock Island in Chicago the proposition that the railroad offer a five-hundred-dollar reward for the arrest and conviction of any person convicted of the destruction of bridges, trestles, cattle guards, crossings, buildings, cars, or other railway property. I suggested one condition, that the Rock Island comply with the ordinances of the cities and build depots meeting those cities' requirements.

Brooks snatched the telegram from Jason's hand. "Don't look so smug. President Cable was adamant in his refusal. Such an agreement would be of no profit to anyone as long as the violence continues against railroad property. I am appealing to the Attorney General and the Secretary of War to help the railroad in its fight against the terrorists."

"It looks like the railroad is like a pig caught under a fence," Jason said. "It's squeal can be heard all over the country."

"Get out of here," Brooks said savagely. "All of you men who have taken this attitude will be damned sorry."

Jason managed to keep his face sober. "Then these gentlemen are free to go?"

"They're free until I order them in here again." His face was raw and violent. "I predict that won't be long."

Jason saw the resentment clouding the three faces. They all had positions of importance, and they weren't used to being talked to like this. He hustled them out of the office before any of them made an unwise remark.

Hager said furiously, "Why did you stop us? We could have told him a few things!"

Jason shook his head. "Sure, and be arrested right there. Brooks is a harassed man. He's growing wild under simultaneous pressure from Washington and the railroad."

A slow grin moved Hager's lips, then he laughed, almost out of control. He pummeled Jason and said, "We've beaten them. They're on the run."

"Listen to me," Jason said sharply. "We're still going to back the law that's been pressed on us, even if we don't like it." He threw up a hand, stopping the protest. "You heard what Brooks said about the Secretary of War. Do you plan to fight the United States Army?"

That sobered them, and Hager reluctantly shook his head. "Looks like we're still hemmed in, doesn't it?"

"It does," Jason said grimly. "We must still religiously avoid doing any harm to railroad property and hope we'll finally win in the courts."

"It ain't fair," Hager said gloomily.

United States Attorney Brooks and United States Marshal Nix of Oklahoma consulted with the Supreme Court. The Court instructed them to request the Secretary of War to send federal troops to Enid and Pond Creek.

"You just better be damned sure that the mail goes through," Brooks ordered. "That's what's made Washington so unhappy."

Nix nodded soberly. At first, he had been in deep sympathy with the people of Enid and Pond Creek, but now he wasn't so sure. This continuing violence got on a man's nerves.

Wasson burst into Jason's office, his face alight with pleasure. "Did you hear what happened, Jason?"

"I've heard so many things that I can't separate truth from rumor," Jason said wearily. "What's your particular bit of news?"

"Judge McAtee has decided he could not sit on a court in Kingfisher. He's referred the case back to L and O counties to be heard before a justice of the peace. I've also heard that Brooks telegraphed Olney that if McAtee does this, we are utterly without power to enforce the law. The depredations against the Rock Island will start all over again. Doesn't that mean we're winning, Jason?"

Jason threw up his hands. "Lord, Mayor, I don't know any more. But I've heard an authentic bit of news. Governor Renfro is meeting President Cable of the Rock Island in Guthrie for a high-level conference. Renfro told me himself."

"Did he know what the coming talk is about?"

Jason debated telling him the meager information he had, then decided Wasson was in this as deep as anybody.

"Not exactly, but he's afraid it could be bad. Cable is unbending. Renfro tried to get him to ease his attitude against Enid and Pond Creek, but he couldn't budge him. I'm going down to Guthrie. If there's any possible way, I'm going to sit in on that conference."

Wasson's face cleared. "That makes me feel a hell of a lot better. Don't let Cable throw his weight around."

"Not if I can help it," Jason said.

CHAPTER TWENTY

Jason met Renfro coming down the street toward the Guthrie Hotel. Jason greeted the man warmly. He liked Renfro and was sincerely convinced that the governor was doing everything in his power for the people of Oklahoma.

"Governor," he said as he shook hands. "Any news about Cable?"

"He's here," Renfro replied. "I'm on my way to talk to him."

"Any idea what's on his mind?"

Renfro shook his head. "Not really. But I've got a bad feeling, Jason. Cable's got a too satisfied look. He's just swallowed a canary, or is getting ready to."

Jason moaned. "Do you think it's all directed at Enid and Pond Creek?"

"That's where his trouble has come from, isn't it? Maybe I'm a pessimist, but I expect the worst."

"Can I talk to him?" Jason pleaded.

Renfro's eyebrows shot up, and he said dubiously, "I don't know, Jason. Nothing was said about an outsider being at the talk. It could get Cable's back up."

"I've got a right to talk for the people of Enid and Pond Creek," Jason persisted.

Renfro gave in. "I don't see where it can do a lot of harm. If Cable's already made up his mind, I don't think your being there is going to change anything."

Just then a man came out of the hotel door. Jason stared after him. He felt he should know this man, but a name wouldn't come.

"Do you recognize him?" Renfro asked.

"I feel like I should," Jason replied.

"That's John Kevan, vice-president of the Rock Island. He's a powerful man. If his position with the railroad isn't authority enough, his relationship to Cable gives him what he lacks."

Suddenly the memory fell into place. Jason had indeed seen Kevan before, but only twice: once the night of the fight in front of the Palace Saloon, and again the next day in the courtroom. No wonder he hadn't recognized him immediately. At both those times Kevan had looked the worse for wear. Now he was all slicked up, and his positive assurance fitted him like a newly fashioned garment.

"What's that relationship?" Jason asked.

"Kevan is Cable's son-in-law," Renfro answered. "Haven't you heard that?"

Jason's eyes rounded. "I'm one of the ignorant kind, Governor. How long ago did he marry Cable's daughter?"

Renfro's forehead knitted as he searched his mind. "About three years ago, I think, but I don't want to be hanged for the accuracy of that. Anyway, Kevan married his position."

Jason was breathing faster, and his eyes were glistening. Now he understood the threat Kevan had made that he would punish Enid and Pond Creek. Was Kevan behind all the trouble? It was entirely possible. With all his power, he was in a perfect position to deal out misery to the town of his embarrassment.

"Maybe I'm clutching at straws, Governor, but I think I've found a lever to move Mr. Cable."

"What is it?" Renfro inquired

"I can't say yet, Governor. Let me see how it goes first."

Renfro studied him. "You've got that stalking look, Jason. If I was Cable, I'd be worried."

"God, I hope you're right, Governor. Ready to have at it?"

Renfro smiled bleakly at him. "As ready as I'll ever be."

The pair climbed the stairs to the third floor. Renfro swallowed hard, then knocked briskly. A man opened it. He was of slight build and had a demeaning expression. Jason had heard descriptions of Cable before, and this man didn't fit them at all.

"Come in and be seated," the man said meekly. "Mr. Cable will be out shortly." He led them to two chairs, then departed.

"Who's he?" Jason asked.

"Never saw him before. One of Cable's servants, I imagine. He carries a retinue wherever he goes."

Jason nodded. That fit Cable's arrogant manner.

Renfro was shifting restlessly by the time twenty minutes had passed. He was really agitated in another ten. "Who the hell does he think he is?" he asked indignantly.

"He's only trying to cut us down to size," Jason said. "He's showing us how unimportant we are. Quit stewing. The longer he makes us wait, the harder I'll hit him."

"I wish I was as sure," Renfro muttered.

The servant came back into the room. "Mr. Cable," he announced. He made it sound as though royalty was about to enter.

Jason lolled in his chair, obviously at ease.

Cable came into the room. He was faultlessly attired, and his chin shone as though excellent barber hands had just finished with him. Renfro started to rise, but Jason reached out, caught his arm, and pressed him back.

"What do you want?" Cable grated. He had a voice tipped with steel. It was the voice of authority, and Jason would bet that few had successfully bucked it.

"Good morning, Mr. Cable," Renfro said. "This is Jason Keeler."

Those steely eyes weighed Jason. "Keeler,

Keeler," he muttered. "I've heard that name before."

"I imagine you have," Jason said dryly. "Keeler of Pond Creek."

Cable's eyes darkened. "I was sure I knew that name. Weren't you involved in the first attack against the Rock Island Railroad? You had a hand in destroying part of our track."

Jason grinned slyly. He had to admire the reach of this man's memory. "Guilty, sir. I—"

Cable abruptly cut him short. "It's a pity you weren't convicted and jailed. It might have stopped some of the outrages that followed."

"I decided to let the courts do my battling after that first incident," Jason replied.

"But that didn't work, either," Cable said mockingly.

"Not so far," Jason admitted. "Too much power in your hands, too much money, too many lackeys willing to obey you."

That enraged Cable. "I've heard enough of this impudence, Governor. I didn't ask for this man in the first place. I demand you dismiss him."

"Not so fast," Jason drawled. "Mr. Cable, you don't realize it, but the Rock Island can be in serious trouble—"

Cable cut him short. "Are you threatening me?" he raged.

"Maybe in a way I am. But I can back it up. Do you love your daughter?"

Cable bristled at the interference in his family affairs. "How dare you?" he stormed. "Mary Ann is none of your affair." He drew a deep breath, and his face purpled. "You've made up my mind for me. I intend to file a civil suit against Enid and Pond Creek for three hundred thousand dollars."

The magnitude of the sum sucked the breath out of Jason. "For what?" he gasped. "I doubt that both towns combined could raise such a sum."

His reaction pleased Cable. "That sum is to compensate the Rock Island for loss in all the depredations your people committed against us, for the destruction of property, rolling stock, and bridges. That doesn't take into account the fear and terror you placed on our employees. I think any court will find that sum eminently fair."

He noticed Jason wasn't wilting at all. He was actually smiling. "Don't you understand what I am saying?" Cable roared.

Jason spoke evenly: "I don't believe the Rock Island can stand all that much unfavorable publicity. What I have in mind would crush your daughter."

Cable breathed hard, and his color wasn't healthy. "How dare you—" he started.

Jason cut him short. "It's unfortunate you allowed your Mary Ann to make such a choice in husbands. You see, your son-in-law used to frequent our saloon, and became very close to

239

the saloon girls. I'm not saying he was intimate with those girls—I'll let him defend himself on that charge. But to all appearances it certainly looked as though he was."

Cable's face reddened, and saliva ran down from the corners of his mouth. He finally managed to get his words out. "If I had a horsewhip, I'd cut you to pieces. How dare you make such an accusation? You heard him, Governor. I call on you to be a witness in the suit I intend pressing on him. I think he'll find defamation of character is still a serious charge."

Jason looked at Renfro and shook his head. "Not if I can prove what I said, sir. There's proof, printed proof. The first time I saw John Kevan, he was fighting with the ladies of the Palace Saloon. One of those ladies had turned John Kevan down as a drinking companion for the evening. It seems he'd visited her several times before and thought he had the right to order her to knuckle under to him. But she didn't want to." Again, Jason shook his head. "A shocking display of bad manners followed when Kevan knocked her down. When I arrived on the scene, six of the ladies had piled on him." He chuckled at the memory. "Believe it or not, they had the advantage. He was a disreputable sight when I rescued him. He made the mistake of trying to hit me, and I knocked him down."

"Liar, liar!" Cable screamed the word over and over.

Jason's grin broadened. "Remember that defamation of character," he warned. "The sheriff was called, and he arrested your son-in-law. He spent the night in jail. The next day he was in court defending himself against the charge of disorderly conduct and disturbing the peace. I'm surprised the story never got to Chicago. It was big in the Enid paper. Your son-in-law was fined and ordered to pay damages for ruining the ladies' dresses. He didn't have that much cash on him and had to wire a Chicago bank for a draft. He spent time in jail waiting for the draft to arrive. At the trial he kept screaming he'd make Enid pay. Was John behind all this trouble? He sounded like a vindictive man."

"You are a—" Cable was on his feet.

Jason advanced toward him. "Don't say it." He stabbed a finger at Cable, and his voice was hard. "I'm tired of being called that word. It won't be difficult to get copies of the paper carrying the story of that trial. I imagine it would crush Mary Ann. What would it do if several copies were sent to your influential people in Washington? I imagine their attitude toward the Rock Island would change drastically."

Cable cringed before Jason's words. "I don't believe you'd do such a thing," he said in a croaking voice.

"I could get a copy of the paper from Enid," Jason said reflectively, "but that would take time. The fastest way to know if I'm telling the truth is to get your son-in-law in here. I think he'd be afraid to lie to you."

Cable called the servant into the room. "Find John," he ordered. "I want him in here immediately!"

Kevan finally appeared, and he was worried. It showed in the furtive shiftiness in his eyes and in the tightness of his mouth. "You wanted to see me, Dad?"

"You're damned right I do! Look around. Do you know either of these gentlemen?"

Kevan's eyes swept across Renfro, then rested on Jason. His Adam's apple rose high into his throat and seemed to stick there. "I don't think I do," he said in a reedy voice.

"You're making it worse for yourself, Kevan," Jason said in an almost pleasant voice. "You know me. Our first meeting was outside the Palace Saloon in Enid. Those girls were mauling the hell out of you when I came up."

"No, no," Kevan said frantically, rocking his head back and forth. "You've got me mixed up with somebody else."

"Do you want me to get proof?" Jason purred. "It's all in the Enid *Wave*. They had a reporter at the trial. He got all the details."

If ever Jason had seen a human being turn into

a trapped rat, he saw one now. Kevan's eyes rolled in his head, his lips trembled, and his hands jerked. Sweat poured off of him, wilting his collar.

Even Cable watching a man go to pieces was shaken. His voice was hoarse when he spoke. "John, this is the time to tell the truth. If you don't, and I find out you're lying, I don't have to tell you how hard it will go for you. Mary Ann was troubled by that draft you drew from your account. You never did tell her what it was for."

"I can tell you," Jason spoke up. "It was for four hundred and fifty dollars, drawn so he could pay his fine."

"That was the amount," Cable said in a dead voice.

Kevan broke under the implied threat. "Dad, it wasn't my fault. I'd been drinking too much. That was the first time I'd been in that saloon. The liquor drove me. I swear nothing happened."

"The first time," Jason said sardonically. "That's not the way Ida Belle tells it." He glanced at Cable. "That's the woman Kevan knocked down. She claimed he'd been there several times before. So much so that he thought he owned her."

Cable put anguished eyes on his son-in-law. "Is that true, John? This is absolutely your last chance."

Kevan broke down and sobbed. He buried his face in his hands, and his shoulders shook. "It was like a madness, sir. The more I saw her, the more the madness grew. I wouldn't have Mary Ann know of this for anything in the world."

Cable straightened in his chair, and some of his dominating air returned. "And I put you in charge of operations through Enid and Pond Creek." He shook his head in disbelief. "I understand now why you came down so hard on those two towns. Get out of here, you lecherous bastard. I'll have another talk with you later."

A beaten man slipped out of the room. Jason could almost pity him. He wouldn't be in Kevan's shoes for anything in the world.

Cable looked at the floor, twisting and pulling at his fingers. "You've made your point," he said dully. "I love Mary Ann too much to put her through this humiliation and shame. I'd do anything to keep her from ever finding out."

Jason laughed easily. "I thought you would."

A full flush of repressed rage colored Cable's cheeks. "What's your proposition?"

"First, you agree in writing there will be no civil suit against Enid or Pond Creek."

Cable's shoulders slumped. "There's more?" he asked, a sarcastic tinge in his voice.

"A lot more," Jason assured him. "The railroad will erect depots and sidings at each town. Each train will stop according to the city's ordinances."

"That's blackmail," Cable screamed.

"A good teacher taught me," Jason said. "That's

what the railroad was doing when they refused both towns the railroad facilities due them."

"Anything else?" Cable asked feebly.

"Yes. Send a telegram to the representative at Topeka. Tell him to withdraw immediately all opposition to Enid and Pond Creek now before Congress. When that bill is killed, you will find that every person opposing the Rock Island will cease activities immediately."

Cable moaned like a wounded animal.

"It's not as bad as you make it sound, Mr. Cable. Haven't you found out already that you are losing a great deal of business on your lines through our towns? Already people are refusing to take passage or ship freight. The Texas cattle business is shifting to the Santa Fe. But you could get all that business back."

Hope flickered in Cable's eyes. "I'll explore this new line of thinking." His voice was still stiff.

"Good," Jason said briskly. "I've always found that when a man gives a few concessions, he is usually showered with benefits." He approached Cable, his hand outthrust. For a moment he didn't think Cable would touch it, but then Cable rose and followed through.

"I was prepared to thoroughly dislike you, Mr. Keeler. I was wrong in that, as I've been in so many things."

Jason grinned and said lightly, "Life is one long

learning experience, Mr. Cable. A man has to reach a certain age before he realizes he has been making mistakes."

Cable bobbed his head. "I know, I know. Maybe more good will come out of this. At least I've saved Mary Ann's marriage." His eyes sparkled. "And, I've gained complete control of my son-in-law. After this, he won't dare think of crossing me."

Jason chuckled. "See, you haven't lost a thing."

Cable eyed Jason with respect. "If you ever think of changing locations, the Rock Island has a place for you. We can always use a man with a head on his shoulders."

Jason briefly considered the proposal, then he shook his head. "I appreciate that offer, sir, but I always like to be my own man."

"I thought you would," Cable said, and there was no rancor in his tone. "The offer's always open, even at a later date."

"I'll keep it in mind," Jason said gravely. He and Renfro shook hands with Cable again, and Cable escorted them to the door.

Outside the hotel, Jason drew a deep breath. "It didn't turn out like I was afraid it might."

Renfro whacked Jason on the back. "Never saw any smoother handling, Jason. You had him eating out of your hand."

Jason smiled. "I just happened to stumble onto the right lever. My God, sir, won't it be good to have a little peace in our part of Oklahoma?"

"It certainly will." Renfro's eyes narrowed as a thought struck him. "When the people find out who's responsible for all this peace, you could run for governor and win. I certainly hope it won't be against me."

"I'll remember that, Governor. I'll wait until you no longer want the job. Now, I've got to get back to Pond Creek and Enid and tell the people that the war with the railroad is over. They can put aside their hostilities and get back to the business of growing with their towns."

He shook hands with Renfro and walked down the street, looking back after half a block. Renfro still stood there, perhaps in an unconscious tribute.

CHAPTER TWENTY-ONE

Derry burst into Jason's office, his eyes wide. "Jason, what's going on? This morning, all the marshals left. Now the soldiers are going, and there's not a single railroad guard left."

"The war's over, Clements," Jason said soberly. "Maybe now things will return to normal."

Derry dubiously shook his head. "I don't think the people will agree with you. They still haven't got what they want."

"They'll get it," Jason assured him. "The railroad is going to build depots in Pond Creek and Enid. From now on, we'll get full service."

"You been drinking?" Derry asked suspiciously.

"I'm sober and sane," Jason said. "I had a long talk with Cable only yesterday. He doesn't think the railroad needs to guard its facilities, so there's no more need for soldiers or marshals."

Derry's suspicions didn't fade. "A complete flipover? That's hard to believe," he said skeptically. "What did you work, a miracle?"

Jason laughed in pleasure. "I didn't work anything. If you're still suspicious, Cable canceled his opposition altogether."

Derry sat down as though his legs refused to support him. "I don't believe it. After all that resistance, what happened?" His eyes narrowed.

"What did you use on him? A form of black-mail?"

"He called it that at first. Didn't Ida Belle tell you of her fight with that railroad man?"

"The one you knocked down?"

Jason nodded. "The same. That was Cable's son-in-law. Cable hadn't heard of the escapade."

"Ah," Derry said as understanding flooded in. "He either withdrew all his opposition or faced publicity that was bound to hurt him."

"I think saving his daughter's marriage was more the reason," Jason said reflectively. "He really loves his daughter. That plus a few other things I pointed out to him. He decided to go back to running the railroad as it should be run."

Derry slapped his knee. "I'll be damned!" he exclaimed. "I always said you were a genius."

"Not a genius," Jason said modestly. "Just lucky. Things just fell my way."

"I'd sure like to stay here," Derry said unhappily. "I've got a feeling you're going to be a big man before you're through. If I tagged along, some of that bigness might rub off on me."

"Ida Belle still determined to leave?"

"More determined than ever. I can't talk her out of it."

"Has anybody been unkind to her, Clements?"

Derry shook his head. "Not openly. Even she admits that. But she claims it's in their eyes, that they're just waiting for the right time to spit at her. You know when a woman gets an idea set in her head it's almost impossible to get it out."

Jason had to agree to that. "Has she set a date to leave?"

"Yes. The end of the week."

"Well, that gives me a little time."

"You don't know Ida Belle."

Jason repressed his smile. Derry was talking to a man who was well versed in the subject of Ida Belle. "I've got to get over to Enid. Want to go?"

"I guess I'd better pass. Ida Belle wants me to buy a few things for the trip." He stood, walked over to Jason, and wrung his hand. "I'm glad you whipped that damned railroad."

"Don't go around crowing about it," Jason said quietly. "We were over a barrel. One little roll and we'd have been crushed. See you when I get back."

He walked into the *Wave*'s office, and Isenberg looked up from his cluttered desk. "What's the good word, Jason?"

"What would you say if I told you the war's over?"

"I wouldn't believe you," Isenberg grunted.

"Haven't you noticed that all the soldiers and the marshals are gone? There are no more railroad guards patrolling the track."

"This some kind of a joke, Keeler?"

"Hardly. The Rock Island has decided to go

back to the business of running a railroad and quit fighting the people." Jason nodded solemnly. "Fact. I talked to Cable recently. He's withdrawn all opposition. He's building depots in Pond Creek and Enid. All trains will stop at each town."

Isenberg feebly shook his head. "It's unbelievable. We've finally won."

"Not we," Jason corrected. "Ida Belle Derry. It was her first resistance to that railroad that started everything. Ida Belle gets all the credit. The people should be grateful to her. I want you to print that."

Isenberg's pencil was already busy, scribbling down a few notes. He had Jason repeat some of his news and asked for more facts about Ida Belle. "How could what she did be that important?"

Jason couldn't tell him all the facts behind the story. That would break his promise to Cable. "Just write that Ida Belle saw the danger in the Rock Island and took the first step to block it. That's all the people need to know."

Isenberg sighed. "You're not going to give me any more, are you?"

"You've got enough to put out an extra. Peace is finally here. What more do you want?"

"Nothing, I guess," Isenberg muttered.

"When will that issue be out?"

"Tomorrow about noon. Is that soon enough?"

"It'll do just fine. Will you send some copies to Pond Creek?"

"Be happy to," Isenberg agreed.

"See you soon," Jason said, and strolled toward the door.

"You made me a promise, April. You agreed to marry me when the trouble with the railroad was over."

A beautiful pinkish color spread across April's face. "I haven't forgotten, Jason. Did you think I wasn't looking forward to that day? It's as important to me as it is to you." A slight touch of dismay crossed her face. "It's just that I have so much to do in such a short time."

"Don't you think I have?" he countered. He had her cornered, and he wasn't going to let her slip away.

"I'll be ready," she whispered.

He kissed her with a new passion. When he finally lifted his head he said, "One other thing, April. Could Ida Belle be your maid of honor?"

April didn't even hesitate. "I'd be delighted. I never even thought of it."

Jason squeezed her hands, pulled her to him, and kissed her again. "Well, you have now. Does two o'clock tomorrow sound all right to you?" At April's nod he said, "Fine. I'll see you then."

• • •

Isenberg was true to his promise. He sent over a lavish number of copies of the *Wave*, and there under a banner headline on the front page was the account of how Ida Belle had throttled the railroad's attempt to choke off Enid and Pond Creek. Jason's eyes were shining when he finished. Isenberg had done a job on that story. He didn't elaborate on just what Ida Belle had done, but he didn't have all the details. He was a skillful writer, and he blew up Ida Belle's part until it sounded more important than Washington's part in saving the country.

Derry and Ida Belle came into the office a few minutes later. Both of them looked astounded.

"What's going on, Jason?" Derry demanded. "We passed more than a dozen people on the way here. Every one of them came up and praised Ida Belle."

Jason grinned. "Have you two read this?" He shoved a copy of the *Wave* toward them.

They read it, their heads together. Ida Belle's eyes were moist, and her lips were trembling when she looked up. "What's this mean? I didn't do anything."

"Have you forgotten John Kevan?" Jason asked gently. "All of what's happened started that night."

"They're thanking me for that?"

"It started with you," Jason said. "Before I forget it, April and I are getting married this

253

afternoon. She wanted me to be sure and tell you that she wants you to be her maid of honor."

He was afraid Ida Belle would break into tears. He moved to her and patted her arm. "Here now! None of that. She wouldn't ask you if she didn't want you."

"But she couldn't," Ida Belle sniffed. "With my background—"

"Stop that kind of talk," Jason said sternly. "That's all in the past and forgotten. Forever."

"How many times have I told you that?" Derry burst in. "Jason is only saying what I tried to say."

Jason waved him quiet. Clements meant well, but sometimes a husband was too close to a wife. "Ida Belle, April wants you."

Ida Belle's eyes filled with tears. She swallowed hard and said pleadingly, "Jason, you're not trying to fool me?"

"Have I ever?" he asked sternly. "You'll find the same feeling exists all through Enid. Now if you're going, you'd better get moving. I've got to hire a hack, dress—" He broke off, grimacing. "There's a million things to do."

Ida Belle's eyes were shining through the tears. "I'll be ready," she whispered. She moved closer to Jason and kissed him full on the mouth.

Derry didn't mind the kiss. In fact, he approved, for he was beaming. But maybe it was just as well that April didn't see it. A woman's forgiveness extended only so far.

Center Point Large Print
600 Brooks Road / PO Box 1
Thorndike, ME 04986-0001 USA

(207) 568-3717

US & Canada:
1 800 929-9108
www.centerpointlargeprint.com